All The Difference A Day Makes

By Nathan Wilson

Chapter One

The mid-morning heavens poured down as the bus
arrived. Jack stood alone at a stop in central Edinburgh,
dressed in a pristine black suit, uneasy in his hangover
because he hadn't seen a single soul since waking there
moments before.

He stared at the driver, who looked an awful lot like his
wife—a doppelganger who refused him any attention; she
just looked ahead.

Intrigued by curiosity, Jack boarded the double-decker
bus to take a better look. However, rather than meeting the
driver, he found himself in a Tudor-style living room with
an open fire to the left that provided the only light. A
window stood tall on the other side with old, heavy
curtains—open to show the moonlit rain of a miserable
northern night.

He guessed he must have still been drunk, though he felt
clear and balanced. It seemed the only logical explanation;
years had passed since he had blacked out and forgotten
chunks of a day, let alone an entire afternoon.

A musky, oaky, smoky bourbon smell teased its way into
his nose and soothed all concern. Jack looked ahead. Two
maroon sofas faced each other by the fireplace.
Mismatched stones built up the walls while black timber
beams ran along the white ceiling. The far wall hid its
history in the shadows, where an old wooden door hung.

"Jack, sit down." a broad-shouldered black man
suggested from one of the sofas. The man was well dressed
in an emerald suede blazer, a white open-neck shirt, black
trousers with a perfect crease down the middle and a pair of

black brogues that shone like a smile on Christmas morning, reflecting the burning fire to the man's right. A lit cigar rested between his ring-wearing fingers. He looked calm and comfortable, sitting back with one leg resting on the other. There was a look of strength about him, a confidence and certainty in his eyes, yet a kindness to his empathetic smile. He could have been around the same age as Jack, maybe a few years older but on the right side of forty.

Jack turned around. The city and the bus had disappeared completely, and instead, a doorway was open that led into a dark corridor with lit candles along the walls.

Bewildered at his amnesia, Jack faced the room, walked towards the empty sofa, and sat with his back to the door. A glass of whiskey rested on the table between the two men.

"The drinks, yours, mate. Now, Jack, I know why you're here, but why don't you tell me yourself? Tell me about it. The whole story. The story of the night. The night your wife died. I'll fill in the bits you weren't… aware of." the man's deep and trusting tone was inviting, even if it was, for Jack, unfamiliar.

Chapter Two

"Well… Earlier that afternoon, I sat at a dining table across from the most stunning redhead the world had probably ever known. Hours later, both her and the mother of my child, who also shared our house, were dead.

The sound of their laughter and the creases in the corners of their smiles haunted me as I walked through an open field in the dark hours of the early morning; it hadn't long been a new day. A loaded rifle rested in my grip as I mourned through the gloom, fearful in my bitterness, for when I returned home just after midnight, the women had been murdered under the moon, and my seven-year-old daughter, Isla, was nowhere to be seen.

There was a gunshot wound over my Mindy's heart as she lay there, still in the same jeans and T-shirt that she was wearing before I left. I crumbled to my knees in complete desolation and looked into her beautiful icy-blue eyes. Eyes that I knew so well. She could speak a thousand words of love without making a single sound. She would say it all with just a look. That look had vanished. She was gone.

A Polaroid photograph was next to my wife's bleeding body as both her and Isla's mother, Cara, lay side by side on the cut grass in the back garden. I knelt beside her, my tears fell onto her face, and I gently picked up the Polaroid.

The photo captured an old and abandoned house that I recognised from the outskirts of the town where we lived, Stamford. It was across the meadowed fields, then on the other side of a river.

I sank completely when I saw the name written on the back of the photograph. ISLA… I knew what I had to do.

Mine and Mindy's bedroom had a chest of wooden drawers with a large hidden compartment at the bottom. After unlocking the compartment, I pulled out an SA80 rifle.

I quickly stripped the weapon, rebuilt it, performed a function test and collimated the rifle's scope before loading it with a magazine of thirty rounds. Once the rifle was cocked and made ready, I fired an aimed shot at the top of the open bedroom door and then reapplied the safety catch.

The neighbours wouldn't have heard or even acknowledged the shot. Not at that hour. We lived on a very wealthy street where the houses were spread out and separated from one another. They were too far away, and my windows were thick with triple-glazed glass. Also, it was such a small and quiet town—peppered with the middle-aged middle class and the elderly. Nothing exciting ever happened. No one would have ever truly suspected it to have been the sound of genuine gunfire. But I couldn't afford to fire a second shot, regardless of my confidence in the surrounding civility.

Two more fully loaded magazines were secured in each jacket pocket, and I slid a further two into each back pocket of my jeans. I grabbed my phone, wallet and keys from the marble kitchen top and swapped my trainers for a pair of Timberland boots.

I didn't lock the house; I just climbed into my car—too angry and eager to get my daughter back, and with the way that the women were killed, it was hard not to fear the worst.

Nobody would have seen me put a rifle in the boot. Our detached house had huge gardens at both the front and the back with trees, fences, and gates that hid the view from potential onlookers, usually only the postmen or a few of the retired dog-walking neighbours. Neither would have been about at that hour. That was one of the attractions I had for the house before buying it, not just the sheer size of it but the privacy.

The drive took no more than five minutes to the meadow's car park, with the only company on the road being the morning chill. I parked up by the side of the meadows. The route I had to walk was known to me. Mindy and I had strolled that way many a time, usually on a Sunday afternoon. The once wondrous walk, immersed with memories of laughter and handheld kisses, had evolved to become the most hellish of nightmares. Sweat dripped. I felt physically sick from the dread and despair, longing for Isla to be safe.

It was nearly a mile from where I parked to the lone-standing abandoned house. I had to go completely unnoticed. The only drivable road that led to the house would have been too obvious; they would have seen me coming. I'd likely be ambushed, and I didn't know what was waiting for me once I got there.

The other way was the backfield route. A walk through the meadows. That's the way I went. They'd likely have expected that too and that I would cross the weir's bridge directly next to the house. What choice did I have? Isla needed me. On foot, I could at least use the cover of darkness to my advantage.

The weirs bridge separated the photographed house from the meadow. I had to cross the river without using the bridge and sneak along the field on the other side of the water where the house stood. There weren't any neighbours for a third of a mile. The house was hidden away and forgotten, with only open grass and water surrounding it— the ideal place to set a trap.

Guided by the moonlight, I trod carefully through the rugged terrain, mindful not to walk off course or trip over, as the grass was halfway up my shin. I could just about see where I was going, but I knew it would be another few minutes until my eyes adapted to the dark.

I looked up at the moon. The sound of my heart beating and the grip of the rifle flooded me with memories of the past.

Seven years before, when I was twenty-nine, I left the Parachute Regiment. I had been an elite infantry soldier in the British Army for six years and had served on meaningfully ferocious tours around the world, mainly in the Middle East. Afterwards, I got involved in arms dealing with Rex, my business partner. He gave me an attractive opportunity to make a lot of money at a time when I wanted to get away from the war to be at home with the girls. I loved being in the military, truly, but when the opportunity presented itself to create a financially free life for my daughter in a world where I could be there for her every day, I took it. I knew the consequences, but Rex's criminal career stretched over twenty-five years. We weren't getting caught; we were too careful.

We mainly dealt with pistols and rifles. There were a few wilder occasions where the buyer wanted something a little extra. That was mental. I was more of the middleman, the courier, if you like, and conducted the quality control. Rex had the connections. They were all over the country, some even international.

Rex was a gangster from Manchester who owned a music bar in the heart of the city. It was an absolute dive that was the place to be for up-and-coming musical talent, and a good way for Rex to wash his money.

Rex and I met when I was eighteen. I had just moved to the city and was a bit of a rock and roller. Completely obsessed with the music, obsessed with the life. I would play in bands around the city and, of course, at Rex's bar while drinking and smoking myself into a world of fantasy. I was a phantom to society.

Rex was one of the toughest men I knew, and I'd been to war. He had weighed over a hundred kilograms since his early twenties. A few months back, we celebrated his forty-ninth birthday. That was a wild night. I'd never seen Mindy so drunk, though she was still effortlessly charming.

Rex was lean, broad and six foot four with a bald head and a big ginger moustache that he put a lot of care and attention into. The ends curled out like handlebars. The charmer's arms were covered in tattooed muscles, and he could ignite fear in groups of aggressors with a pair of the scariest eyes you'd ever seen.

A few men worked for him, but he wasn't in charge of the city's top gang—the O'Briens were. They kept out of each other's way. There was a truce in the city, and they did their best not to step on each other's toes. It had been years since the rivals had had a proper fallout.

A few hours before I found the Polaroid, I had met with Rex in Nottingham to discuss a deal with a Russian geezer, who was also mental, really, a proper nutter. Then, I drove back home to Stamford. That's when I saw them on the garden grass. They were just lying there. If it weren't for the blood, you probably wouldn't have been able to tell they were dead. Still just as beautiful as ever, the pair of them.

My wife Mindy and I met one afternoon when I was twenty-eight. Both Mindy and Cara were twenty-four at the time. It was a drunken night out in London that ended with me going back to their hotel. In the early hours, after the sex, Mindy and I stayed up drinking some more, laughing on the floor while Cara was asleep in bed.

Mindy was dreamy, perfect in every way. She was funny, smart, astonishingly beautiful, and had the most incredible copper-coloured hair that could make it all warm and cosy on the coldest of days.

We grew closer over the following weeks after that weekend in London. She was heartbroken when she learned that Cara had fallen pregnant from the night the three of us had spent together in the hotel room. Mindy and Cara had been best friends since they were little girls, and her best friend was mothering the child of her lover.

It was complicated, and a little difficult to begin with, but only for the first few weeks, then it got easier. The girls were too close to let it get between them. They were almost like sisters. Cara was even the maid of honour at our wedding a couple of months after Isla was born.

I bought a house in Stamford, the town the girls were from, and we all moved in together. It was weirdly perfect. Mindy adored her stepdaughter as if she was her own. And Cara couldn't have been more in love with the situation, truly. There was nothing between Cara and me at all. She was beautiful, stunning in fact, but she grew to become like family to me—the sister I never had. There wasn't a jealous bone in either of their bodies. It was our family. The only family I had ever felt a part of.

My mum walked out on my drunk of a dad when I was a little lad. I'm not sure what happened to her. I hadn't spoken to him either since I was eighteen. He was a waste of space my whole childhood. I pretty much brought myself up. I don't even know if the man lived in the same place...

In the meadowed field, my eyes had adapted well to the dark of night. I'd covered over a third of my journey. It wouldn't be long until I had to cross the river.

As I walked further, I felt my phone vibrate in my jeans pocket. I pulled out my mobile and took a knee. A withheld number was calling me. I answered and put the phone to my ear.

For a few seconds, there was silence, apart from the creepy sound of loud breathing on the other end of the call. Then, history started to repeat itself. That haunting rendition. Someone started to whistle the melody of the famous song 'Dirty Old Town' down the line. The hairs stood up on the back of my neck. That exact call had happened before. However, the last time was fourteen years prior, when I was twenty-two. That was another week when everything seemed to go the other way."

Chapter Three

"In 2007, roughly fourteen years before the night Mindy was killed, I was sat alone on the floor, surrounded by an abundance of cash. A couple of thousand, it looked to be.

There must have been a fight; from experience, I had taken on a few of them.

Only moments before, I had woken naked on the living room floor of my city-centre flat. The bustling noise of a busy Mancunian morning burst through the windows from below. Car horns, roadworks, and loud shoppers filled the streets of a T-shirt-wearing Saturday.

Surrounded by broken glass and crockery, I stared at my blemished hands and blood-stained skin. My knees, shins and elbows were cut and bruised. The knuckles on my right hand showed open wounds and the reassurance of getting a few decent punches in. My brain spun like a broken fairground ride as a disgusting hangover cut through the back of my eyeballs. I had been hit on the left side of my face with something heavy and pole-like. My nose was bloody, and my lip was split with the taste of blood and alcohol fermenting my breath.

I hobbled over from the living area to a pot-filled kitchen sink in the far corner of the room. It was hard not to tread on the broken mess below. I reached out to turn on the cold tap and gently picked up a dirty wine glass from the washing-up pile. There was no effort made to wash away the staining residue of the red wine that I had drank the day before, nor did I wait for the tap to turn icy cold, yet the water tasted like nothing could have been sweeter.

I turned around. A black leather sofa sat against a long-sided wall to my right. An upside-down paint-splattered table was about a meter directly in front of me. The chair was on the other side of the room. Paper, paints and brushes were scattered around the place. To the far corner of the room, on the left, there was a desk that had on it a large, cracked mirror and a CD player. Some things were scattered on the floor below, like pairs of sunglasses, CDs, books, lighters, and guitar plectrums. My three guitars were in the other corner with an amplifier on its side.

Paintings were displayed across the walls of the kitchen-living room combo, like some sort of slightly shit avant-garde French art gallery. They warmed the room with vibrant and abstract patterns of colour. Above the sofa, two of my favourite paintings were hanging half destroyed. That was all from the mystery of the previous night's drinking. I was so relieved to see that the one of the mysterious marine monster avoided it all. Mona, my girlfriend at the time, would have gone off her head if that one had been ripped in any way. She painted it.

Like a wounded sailor, I staggered out of the room and into the small square hallway. My hand reached out to the left to try the front door handle. To add to the horror, I found that it was unlocked. Anxiety spiralled as my head descended a studded helter-skelter. That had never happened before, no matter what drunken state I had been in. I was a little bit obsessive about making sure that the doors were locked, regardless of how drunk the night got.

I sat on the floor for a minute, with my battered head in my blood-stained hands, trying to puzzle together the pieces. Where had all the money I'd woken up to come from? Who had I been fighting with? Did the fight happen in my living room? Why was I naked? Where were the clothes that I was wearing?

My phone rang from the living room. I got to my feet, hoping it was Mona, and limped over to my phone, which was under the sofa, while again trying to avoid the mess on the floor. I felt a shiver of concern. An unknown number was calling. I looked at it for a moment, letting it ring and ring in my hand before answering. I put the phone to my ear without saying a word. The breathing from whoever was calling was aggressive. Then, the whistling began. That familiar tune. That chilling rendition. Slow and sinister. 'A Dirty Old Town'.

My bloodied finger ended the call after just a few lines of melody. My head was too freaked out with the state I'd woken up to and way too hungover to entertain the lunacy.

The time was nearly half past eleven in the morning. A walk over to the fridge for a cold beer was needed. The hair of the dog to sort out my pain. After finishing the beer in one effort, I was cracking open another can when the withheld number rang again. There was no chance of answering a second time. So I took a swig of my beer, turned my phone off and walked out of the living room and into the bathroom to take a shower.

That was when I saw my face in the mirror's reflection for the first time. I looked a mess.

After turning on the shower and letting the water run, I wiped the blood away from my face with a towel that had just been dampened from the sink. It hurt a lot. Steam began to fill the room.

With most of the blood off my face, I got into the shower. The stinging got worse when the hot water fell onto my broken skin. While washing my hair, it was hard not to notice the puddle of red surrounding the strands that had fallen from my head. Checking over my injuries, I knew there would be a full recovery in just a few days. There were bruises and scratches, nothing was broken—no need for any stitches.

I felt a lot better when I was out of the shower and dressed with clean teeth. The smallest amount of styling cream was ruffled into my hair to mess it up a little. My phone was in my jeans pocket. I'd not bothered to turn it on again as I knew Mona would have called sooner or later with agitated questions about the night before, and there were no answers for her.

By that point, I had finished my second beer and was halfway through my third, which was doing the job and fixing my hangover. The laces of my trainers were tied. I was sitting on the sofa, staring at the broken plates and the piles of cash in front of me.

From just before midnight until I woke up that morning, memory had escaped me completely. Mo, Mona, and Katie were with me; that much was known. But where did everyone end up? And why wasn't Mona at the flat? It was rare for Mona and me not to wake up together after a night out.

Out of nowhere, the front door burst open, and three men came charging in, screaming to get on the ground. I didn't move; I just stared at them, startled, and took another swig of my beer. Two of them then grabbed me. My nearly finished beer fell to the floor as they dragged me out of the flat. I shouted at them, asking what it was all about, but got no reply. The third man stood looking at the mess on the floor and helped himself to a few quid, stuffing the notes in his pockets before leaving with the rest of us.

These men were not strangers; they weren't friends either. They worked for Rex as his henchmen. Rex had a few other thugs who worked for him, too.

The two carrying me threw me in the back seat of their Land Rover, parked outside my flat's entrance, hidden from civilian sight. They sat on either side, squashing me with their body heat.

The pair were only a few years older, maybe around twenty-five, and were big lads, real bruisers—broad and aggressive. I'd seen them before, but I didn't know their names. The man sitting to my left was a black man with a shaved head. He was wearing jeans and a black T-shirt. He had a gold chain around his neck and a fancy wristwatch to match. The man to my right was white with short and spiky dark hair. He was wearing a black Puma tracksuit, zipped up to the top.

The third man was John. John was Rex's right-hand man. His number two. He was in his early thirties, slim-built and well-trained in a mix of martial arts. He had a blonde, side parted comb over and always wore black suit trousers with a short-sleeved shirt tucked in. The shirt was usually unbuttoned to just above his belly button so that you could see the white vest that he wore beneath. He had tattoos up his arms and forever had a cigarette on the go. There was a big scar running down his left cheek. No one was sure how he got it. The stories varied. Most, of course, were made up. They were mental tales.

Some say he fought a dozen Barcelona fans on his own after a mid-week Champions League match and came out as the victor. Others say he stuck his head out of his car while driving and head-butted a motorcyclist who overtook him a mile or so back. Others say he cut it himself with a knife moments before a street fight to intimidate the rivals. The stories were nonsense, total bullshit, but John was an absolute nutter, and somehow all the stories you could imagine being true. He didn't like to talk about the scar. The last man who joked about it lost his front teeth. John headbutted him.

John got in the front seat and lit a cigarette. Then we drove off through the city centre. The atmosphere was vibrant around the streets. People were everywhere—just another normal Saturday in Manchester for most.

It didn't take long to get to Rex's city centre bar in the Northern Quarter. John's Land Rover drove down a back road behind the bar's street. There must have been a fire there the night before. A car was half burned out and pretty much written off from the inferno.

The Land Rover pulled up by the fire exit. John and the other two thugs opened their doors and got out. The Puma tracksuit man dragged me out with him. I protested that I could walk, but they were having none of it. Both the thugs pretty much carried me into the bar while John swagged along behind, still smoking.

I was taken down to the basement and tied with rope to a chair that faced the stairs we'd just come down. I'd been down there many times before when I used to work for Rex a few years back on the bar.

Above me was a dim, dirty light bulb dangling from the ceiling. There were dozens of beer barrels around the place; a few were piped up to the pumps. Damp cases of wine and spirits were elevated off the grim and wet floor in the corner on wooden pallets. It was horrific down there. Cigarette ends were everywhere. The walls were dark, old and full of cobwebs. It smelled of rust, sweat and piss. A few puddles were dotted around that I doubted even a rat would bathe in. The true horrors, though, were hidden in the shadows.

When John lit another cigarette, the light produced from his Zippo's flame briefly showed the decorated despair and mould around the walls. I asked him if I could pinch a smoke. He just looked at me in silence with a thousand-yard stare. Then, the thug in the Puma tracksuit punched me around the face, catching my mouth with his swing. I would have been knocked to the ground if it wasn't for the rope. My head dangled down towards the floor. It hurt, but I didn't want to let him know that, so I lifted my head to face him, trying not to look defeated. Blood dripped from my mouth. I spat it in the direction of his trainers and smiled at him provocatively. Then, the other thug in the black T-shirt punched me around the other side of the face. That one caught me on the right cheek. My ear started to buzz a singular note loudly. I stared at the floor, again slumped over the rope, while blood dripped from my mouth onto the ground.

I knew Mona would have a fit when she saw me like that. I wasn't quite sure how I was going to explain everything, although I knew she wouldn't have been surprised. Trouble always seemed to have a way of finding me. Throughout the three years, she'd become no stranger to picking up the pieces of my drunken ways. And to be honest, she were pretty mental herself, even without the drink.

The sound of heavy boots casually strolled across the floorboards above us and made their way down the stairs that I was facing. Rex's giant stature stood before me at the doorway—a silhouette of strength.

'What you staring at, ya pervert?' Rex had a thing for calling everyone a pervert.

Rex was a big name around the city. His ferocious reputation meant he was feared across the northwest of England, with connections, friends and enemies in most cities, up and down the country. He was a no-nonsense drug dealer of weed and ecstasy. A hardened aggressor that would stand toe to toe with anyone for a fight. In his youth and early twenties, he was a well-respected local boxer and a bit of a thief.

The thirty-five-year-old had no wife or children. The women, however, loved him, and he loved the women. He was a bit of a looker, a handsome and confident bloke—an artist of charisma who could charm his way into the hearts of the taken and wedded.

Before his mum died, he always made sure that she was alright and looked after her financially, especially after his dad went to prison for armed robbery and got his time extended for a fight with the guards.

The size of the man was spooky. He had giant, rough hands, a huge gorilla-like back, and legs the size of tree trunks. On that day, he was wearing a white vest tucked into his jeans so that you could see the tattoos on his colossal arms.

'Fucking hell, boys, you weren't meant to fill him in that bad. Jack, you look like shit.' the huge man said, to which

John explained that they had found me looking that way and that the boys had only hit me twice for being a cheeky prick.

'Quite the night you've had then, haven't ya? Ya little pervert. Do you know why you're down here? Knobhead. Bit of a car pervert, are ya? Think you're Guy fucking Fawkes or some prick from the Prodigy? I ought to do you right now. Slay you where you fucking sit. Cut out your eyes and those pretty little girly lips and...'

'Is that a song?' I jumped in with a mouth full of blood before he could finish what he was saying. Rex smiled.

'Who's done that to you anyway? Want me to do them in for ya?' Rex always had a bit of a soft spot for me. I think he almost saw me like the son he never had. He'd done loads for me over the years, watched over me, and given me a job at the bar when I first moved to the city four years before.

'Rex, why am I here? What's with the rope?' I asked him while John blew cigarette smoke in my direction.

'You really don't know what this is all about, do ya? Fucking hell, Jack. Well, you, you little pervert, took a walk round the back here last night and had a piss up the side of Ricky's car. Then you threw your fucking ciggie through the driver's window. The whole thing went up like some Klan pervert was having a barbie. Fucking lucky the boys got to it before it spread. You little knobhead. Ricky wants you dead. We saw it were you from the CCTV... bellend! I've talked to him. Calmed the pervert down. Said I'd deal with it. I don't know why that thick twat left his windows down... Anyway, I digress. You, ya little knobhead, you're gonna get Ricky a new car. A half-decent one as well. Not no shitty banger. A popper runner. You've got a week. One week from today. No exceptions. If you don't come up with a motor within the time, we've agreed he can kick your fucking teeth in. Fairs fair. A fucking week, Jack. Done. Now, fuck off. Make sure he understands boys, but not too hard; he looks like he had enough last night.' Rex turned back around and walked up the stairs to the bar.

I didn't know much about Ricky. All I knew was that he was an older geezer who worked for Rex and wasn't a bloke to mess with.

John then took a drag of his cigarette and side-kicked me in the chest like some ninja. I fell backwards with the chair and hit my head on the soggy ground. The back of my hair soaked up a lot of it. I'm almost certain that some of it could have been piss. The smell was vile.

The two thugs then picked me and the chair back up, and the Puma tracksuit-wearing chav held my head. John threw his cigarette on the floor and then punched me in the face. It hurt a lot more than the first two. The Puma tracksuit thug let go, and my head dangled downwards again. Blood trickled onto my knees. Then the Puma tracksuit lad hit me around the face himself twice.

The T-shirt-wearing thug untied me and told me to stand up. I slowly got to my feet and tried my hardest to stand tall and look undefeated. At that moment, John shin kicked me on the side of the left thigh, just above the knee, Muay Thai style. My leg dropped, and I fell to my knees in a shallow puddle. The Puma tracksuit thug then punched me in the stomach and then around the face. I fell to the floor in a heap. I lay there while the three men left the basement and walked up the stairs, laughing. I could hear John clicking his lighter to smoke another cigarette.

I stayed in the dirt for a moment and thought that just the day before, I was talking on the phone to Mona about maybe going abroad to Spain for a holiday. Twenty-four hours later, I was laying in piss, I'd been beaten up twice, and I owed Ricky a car.

I got to my feet. My clothes were damp and dirty. My left leg was in rag, it was in complete agony, everywhere was. I could barely hobble as I climbed the creaky stairs, clinging to the railing for support. At every step, there was a flare of pain from a different body part.

At the top of the stairs, I turned left to walk into the main bar. There was a stage to my right, where I had performed numerous times. It was still set up with a drum shell and the guitar amplifiers from whichever band had played there the night before. The cleaner hadn't been in yet. There were still beer spillages and small fragments of broken glass on the dance floor. Looking left, on the other side of the bar in the far corner, sitting alone was Rex. He was smoking a cigarette and drinking a bottle of beer. A second bottle was opposite him on the table.

'Come here, ya little pervert.' he called out to me.

I hobbled over and sat opposite. He gestured with his hand that the other bottle was mine. I took a swig. It was deliciously cold and gently stung the sores inside my mouth. He then pushed his pack of cigarettes forward to insinuate that I could have one. I took one out of the packet, put it to my lips and sparked a flame.

'You should really get a grip of your drinking, Jack.' Rex said before taking a big swig of his bottle. I looked at my beer and smiled.

'You seem to be helping me towards the path of righteousness.'

There was a pause, and then we both laughed and had a drink.

'I'm not forcing ya. You make your own choices in life, lad. When that Devil pervert tempted Jesus in the desert to turn some stones into fucking bread after he'd not eaten for days, he told him where to go, son. Said on ya bike, Lucy lad, I'd rather fucking not.'

'Rex, you're a drug dealer, mate.'

'That's beside the point, you little pervert.' he said. 'You chose, and you will continue to choose. It's your life. You are the captain that steers the fucking vessel of circumstance. Your future is a direct reaction to the actions you make today and each day going fucking forward, mate. Exhibit A. You were a little knobhead last night, so therefore, today, you are fucked, my friend. However, the beauty of humanity is that we have the ability to change the course of our reality, to steer that ship towards practically anywhere we want. Or you could steer that ship right the other way. The choice is yours. Yeah, I gave you a beer; I thought it would help with the pain. You seen yourself? Fucked, mate. Anyway, under normal circumstances, I would of sparked one up, but you need your head screwed on right now. You need to come up with a plan, Jack. A plan to get that car, or you are well truly fucked.'

I didn't reply and just let what Rex had said sink in while I continued to smoke. I didn't tell him about the money I'd woken up to. Normally, I would have. Normally, I told Rex pretty much everything.

After a little thinking, I decided it would have been stupid to use that money in the flat to buy a car. I still didn't know where the money had come from, and I was concerned that using the money would highlight the fact that there was a few thousand pounds of blood-stained cash lying about my flat while the owners were out there looking for it.

Also, my bank account was near enough empty with my rent money going out the other day. Rex was right; a plan was needed, and fast.

'You'll be alright, Jack.' Rex told me. 'You'll make it one way or the other. You've got that… perviness about ya. A sort of aura… Have always thought that… Right anyway, you little knobhead, you need to fuck off. I've got shit to do today, and so have you. Have a good one, and stay outta trouble. Go on, fuck off. Call me if you need me.'

With that, I got to my feet, nodded to Rex, then turned and staggered out of the bar's front door.

The instant I walked outside, the heat of the summer sun hit me. I turned left and walked down the street towards the city centre. People stared with taunted bewilders as sweat ran down my face and into my bloodied wounds. When reaching a bin on the side of the road, I put my empty beer bottle in it and threw my cigarette end away.

Piccadilly Gardens was my destination. It was bustling with people, thousands and thousands, like always. People must have thought I looked mental. I could have hardly blamed them.

My plan was to catch a bus to Mo's house.

Mo was my best mate. He grew up a Muslim, and even though he was still a firm spiritual believer, he hadn't been to a mosque since he did mushrooms while listening to Led Zeppelin for the first time when he was fifteen. Since then, he mainly worshipped the rock and the roll. His family resented him for that. They didn't speak much. They were an incredibly traditional Indian family, and Mo was the biggest stoner I knew. He grew weed in his fucking wardrobe.

The hippy was a couple of years older than me—a tall, skinny man with long dark hair. In the time that we'd known each other, I'd only seen him without a pair of circular rose-tinted glasses on maybe three times, even at night. The bearded rocker always wore one of his baggy, multi-coloured collarless shirts with black skinny jeans and some knackered, multi-coloured Air Max's that he'd had for years.

We met at Rex's bar one night not long after I moved to the city and hit it off straight away, becoming friends instantly. He was the coolest guy I knew and had a heart of gold. He got along with absolutely everyone and would talk to anyone. He was also one of the best bass guitar players that I'd ever come across. We played in the same band together for a couple of years, but it wasn't that serious a band. The drummer was always off with his girlfriend in a realm away from reality.

Mo was a man of the people. He always had stories of the madness he'd gotten up to the night before with such and such or the crazy drugs he had ended up taking with so and so at the most random of places around the city. It used to blow my mind when we would bump into a stranger in the street who would confirm one of his tales. Everyone knew him. I felt proud to be able to call him my best friend. I wouldn't tell him that, though, unless I was really drunk.

The loveable hippy was a very calming, selfless and funny dude with a genuine interest in everything anyone said. We never fell out once, and I never caught his character in a moment of hostility. He would always help anyone and everyone. I loved him like a brother.

Mo lived in a bedroom in a shared house in Rusholme, Manchester, just over a mile out of the city centre. He didn't work; instead, he collected benefits each month and sold a bit of weed here and there. He was a simple man with simple needs.

A young and malnourished bus driver at Piccadilly Gardens wouldn't let me board looking like I did, so I had to walk. I didn't mind; it gave me time to think things through in the fresh air, and the longer I walked, the less my leg hurt. The summer sun kissed my wounds and stung them in the gentlest of ways. The continued tormented looks in my direction from the thousands of strangers I passed didn't bother me; I was too caught up in a world of my own, trying to piece together the problematic events of the night before.

Taking the turn to reach Mo's rundown street, I could see him outside his front gate. He was halfway down the road, talking to a man, and appeared to be in deep conversation. It was only when I'd gotten a little closer that I realised that the man Mo was talking to was homeless. They were sharing a smoke. Most probably a joint. Mo looked very excited to see me.

'My dude.' Mo said. 'I've messaged you twice. Where've you been, bro? This here is Lez. Lez is a real gent. Lez bro, meet Jack. Jack, meet… what the fuck happened to your face, man?'

'Alright, Mo. I was hoping you could fill me in on that, actually. I've got a bit of a problem, too.' I replied to the happy hippy.

'I've got you covered, my dude. Lucy, from the ground floor of the house, has loads of creams and maybe has some suppositories, too, man. You'll be sound in no time. Lez, my friend, you'll have to excuse us. Keep the smoke, man. Come on in, Jack, let's get you sorted.'

'No, you fucking idiot, I don't have…'

'I know, I know. I was just having a laugh, my dude— just a joke. Come on inside, man. Lez, safe, bro.'

I nodded to Lez as we walked past to go into Mo's house.

It was a strange house, a little bit like a student house on steroids. No one who lived there was a student, yet they all lived like one. I don't think any of them worked. There were crisp packets, lighters, rolling papers and ashtrays along the hallway floor, and the magnolia walls always looked dirty and smoke-stained, with the occasional political message graffitied along the way. Most of the time, there would be random people walking about and different types of music playing from each bedroom. It was like an after-party that started a few years ago and had never stopped.

We went up the stairs to Mo's bedroom. Inside, sitting on his bed, was Katie. Katie was a good friend of ours. She was Mona's best friend. Her long blonde hair fell over her shoulder. She was always stunningly overdressed as if she'd fallen out of a time machine from the 1960s. I think Mo had been in love with her for some time, but he'd never said anything about it, and nothing had ever happened between them.

I sat on one of his two bean bags on the floor while Mo took his place in his chair. He had one of those reclining grandfather chairs with a retractable table attached.

His room was always oddly clean and obviously stunk of weed. There were psychedelic tapestries pinned all over the walls. He'd switched his light bulb for a red one, so the room had a sort of seductive and psychedelic glow. He didn't have a television; he just had a CD player with a huge collection of CDs piled by its side. At that moment, Jimi Hendrix was playing, a track called 'Third Stone from the Sun'. There were a few bongs on his desk and a stack of books on ancient history, psychedelic drugs and some medieval fantasy novels. A mini fridge was underneath that just had beer and cheese in it, and an incense stick was almost constantly burning on top of a bass guitar amp. Two bass guitars were in the corner next to his weed-growing wardrobe, with a set of drawers to the side where he kept his clean clothes.

Mo told me to grab three beers from the fridge. I handed one each to him and Katie. The hippy then began rolling a spliff while explaining that the last time he had seen me was just before one in the morning, and Mona was still with him and Katie until half past two. Then she left the bar to go home. Apparently, I just went missing. No one could get hold of me, and no one had any idea where I had gone. It usually was Mo that went missing, often after consuming too many psychedelic drugs.

I started to fill Mo and Katie in on what I knew about waking up naked to loads of cash and having been beaten up or at least being involved in a fight. And that Rex's lads turned up at the flat to kidnap me. Mo passed the spliff around. We each took three drags and then passed it to the person on the left.

'Jack, what the fuck? You're absolutely mental. Lovely,

but mental. I'm just happy you're okay.' said Katie, who was shocked but not surprised by the story. Mo nodded in agreement.

'What are you going to do?' she added. I really had no idea and told her that with a shrug of the shoulders.

After a moment's silence, Mo smiled excitedly and suggested a glimmer of hope.

'Jack, my dude. I have a plan!'"

Chapter Four

"2004...

Acrylic nails gently stroked my head as I woke. I was still drunk. The sort of morning drunk that could combat all insecurities and any hangover. My eyes slowly opened to a realisation. It was not my room.

I looked at the stranger stroking my hair. Fucking hell. I lost all interest for reason—nothing that troubled me a few seconds before played any involvement in the present. The verve for the gifted circumstance overruled the fear of drunken dubiety. All I could think of was how beautiful the woman in bed with me was.

Long, dark, and curly hair fell over her heart-shaped face. Big, happy, brown, doe-like eyes gazed through me as if I'd known her all my life. She was smiling like a giddy schoolgirl. Her perfect red lips couldn't conceal her crystal-like white teeth as the creases in her dimples provoked every impulse in my pathetically smitten body. I was enamoured and immersed completely in her beauty.

I brushed the hair behind her ear. A thin, silver necklace with a green shamrock on the end hung around her olive skin. Our naked legs were intertwined. Her lips softly kissed my neck as my hand ran down her silky back.

There was almost no doubt of the happenings of the night before. Unfortunately for me, though, I couldn't remember the sex at all. I couldn't remember a thing. Anything past leaving Rex's bar with Mo to go to a club in Deansgate just after midnight was erased from my memory. However, there was no chance that I was going to forget the sex from the morning.

Once we finished, she lay with her head on my chest. Both of our bodies rushed with blood as our hearts worked on overload, trying to catch back the breath that had been stolen by compulsion. It felt as if my aortas were about to sprout from my chest. Sweat and scratches ran down my skin. Bite marks gently burned my lips. She was heavenly.

She kissed me on the chest and then sat up to reach over to her bedside table, from which she grabbed a pack of cigarettes, a lighter and an ashtray. A cigarette was pulled out and put to my lips before she kissed me on the cheek and lit a flame so that I could smoke. After mine was lit, she sat back and sparked her own. The young woman sat there, smoking, smiling, and stroking her neck, giddy and blushful in her pride.

'Jack, what happened to your friend?' the bronze beauty asked me softly.

She knew my name. I hadn't a clue what hers was, not the faintest idea or anything about her other than the fact that she was an absolute stunner. Were we even still in Manchester? The morning sky outside suggested that we were. Or maybe I'd died. I teased that idea around my head for a moment. I was dead, and there were angels in heaven with pink bedrooms. It clearly fucking rained a lot in heaven too.

'Who Mo? A lot of drugs.' She laughed at my response.

'No. I could work out that much. He's lovely, though. Very sweet. But what happened to him? Where did he go? He just… disappeared. You two were so funny.'

I wasn't dead. Maybe if I were less drunk, I'd have been a little more embarrassed.

'Where Mo goes, no one ever really knows. Sometimes, he just vanishes. He's a wandering, wondrous flower child, bohemian to the beat of man. An oracle devoted to the one-night stand, and a very giving lover, so I'm told.'

Her smile turned to a look of hurt, and her eyes changed to resemble those of a predator of assassins. A puff of smoke clouded from her cigarette-smoking mouth as her innocent and pure posture evolved to become an anatomy of strength and certainty.

'That wasn't what this was, was it?... A one-night stand?' she asked both dolefully and indignantly.

I knew it was too good to be true. She was fucking mental. There's no way someone could get away with being that beautiful without something else being a little off. I didn't even know her name, yet I could see in her infuriation the imagery of her fatally setting fire to a white wedding dress that she was wearing while I was tied up and bleeding to death in the corner of a church, surrounded by rose petals and petrol. I had gone from floating in the clouds of calm to falling out of the sky and drowning in a fiery sea, surrounded by sharks and being showered with the fragments of a broken hourglass that marked my time in heaven over.

My silence was only exacerbating further. She looked fucking mental. Scary, like her eyes had become possessed by a storm.

'What's my name?' she asked. Her perfect boobs distracted me further.

'Your name? What? That's such a mad thing to ask.' I said with a soft laugh, trying hard not to seem nervous or uncomfortable. It was obviously a lie. I couldn't even think of what letter her name began with.

'What's my fucking name, Jack?!' the psycho asked again, that time more aggressively.

There was a moment's pause as we looked each other in the eye. I was half smiling as a coping mechanism for the awkwardness. The bronze beauty wasn't smiling, though she still looked astonishingly pretty—almost cat-like. No matter how angry she got, there was still a gorgeousness to her that pulled you in.

Then she docked her cigarette out in the ashtray and leant forward towards my naked torso, looking me in the eyes while she did so, glaring with a dominant and seductive confidence. Her head looked to my body, and with her index finger, she slowly began to scratch out the letter M with her nail into my chest. I wouldn't say it hurt, but it was aggressive, and I think it was intended to cause pain. It was followed by the letter O, then an N, and finally A. Mona.

'You wasn't meant to like that.' Mona whispered while taking my cigarette end off me and returning the ashtray to the bedside table. I didn't know what she meant until she knelt back off me to reveal that I had made the firmest of tents in the bed sheets. Mona smiled.

'What do we have under here then?' she whispered excitedly.

Mona pulled back the bed sheet and leaned forward so that her head was on my crotch. Her back was arched so that her bum was in the air, like a cat about to pounce. Then she... well, let's just say I don't know how she could ever look her mother or father in the eye again after doing what she did next, not with her having mastered those sorts of acts. The acts of the erotic arts. The way she used her mouth on me made me certain that she would turn to dust if she ever tried to enter a church. Fucking hell. I didn't know anyone could do that with their mouth. And how did she do that thing with her tongue? I'd never finished so quickly... I definitely wanted another one of those.

Mona then climbed on top of me and started riding me like a possessed cowgirl, whispering aggressively in my ear.

'What's my name?'

'Mona.' I whispered back as the sex got more intense. She slapped me on my marked chest.

'Say it louder!'

'Mona.' I whispered a little louder. She slapped me again, that time harder.

'Say it fucking louder!'

'Mona.'

'Fucking louder!' she groaned.

I rolled us over so that I was on top. Her legs tied themselves around my hips, and her nails scratched long marks up and down my back as she moaned more and more while begging me to say her name over and over again.

I pulled out just in time; thank fuck.

Mona held me tightly, squeezing me with her arms and barely able to catch her breath.

'I love you.' she whispered in my ear. What the actual fuck? Red flag! Big fucking red flag! Why would she say something like that? We'd just met.

But then again, she was unbelievably beautiful. Maybe the most stunning woman I'd ever seen, ever. And... well, she did that thing with her mouth. That was good. Really good. A bit too good.

Her hairless body was perfect. She had a tiny waist and a huge, perky bum. Her natural sweet scent as well, it drew me in. I couldn't get enough of it.

I did feel kind of... I'm not sure, but hugging her just felt right. We fit into each other like a jigsaw. Her soft and warm skin was so inviting. There was an acoustic guitar in the corner of her room, too. That was surely a good sign?

Suddenly, there was a knock on the bedroom door.

'Mona, do you want any breakfast, love?'

'Coming.' Mona replied happily to the voice on the other side of the door.

'Oh yes, you get to meet my parents!' Mona said excitedly in my ear. Shit...

We got out of bed and started getting dressed. Mona's smile was beaming from ear to ear as she skipped across the room to retrieve her pink pyjamas from a chest of drawers next to her large wardrobe with mirrors for doors.

Looking around the room, I noticed a massive poster of Fleetwood Mac on one wall and various paintings that I later learned she had done herself. They were incredible. There was a desk against another wall with a turntable on top of it with several vinyl records in a neat pile to the side.

A large mirror lay against the wall on top of the desk with an assortment of makeup and pots of cream in front of it. Paints, paint brushes and sketch pads were on the floor. On the windowsill, there were three plants and a bookcase below it with an extensive collection of CDs.

Then I saw it. On top of the bookcase. Fuck. There was a stuffed teddy bear with its head half hanging off. Jesus. Another red flag. Why had she done that?

I put my black jeans on and then checked my pockets. I still had my keys; that was good. Then I checked for my phone. My phone wasn't there.

'Mona, have you seen my phone or my shirt?'

'Yes, you said my name! Your shirt is over there, and you said you'd lost your phone last night. It was why you couldn't take my number.' Mona replied excitedly while running up to kiss me on the cheek.

I half-remembered losing my phone. Standing up, I looked at the shirt in the corner of her room.

'That's not my shirt?'

'It's the one you were wearing last night.'

I walked over to the shirt and picked it up. It was a red suede shirt with missing buttons. Whose shirt was it? Where had I gotten it from?

'There's no buttons on this shirt?' I told her.

'Yeah, you ripped it open while dancing on top of a table, and they all came off. Then you spent the whole night walking around with it undone. I thought you looked great; I couldn't keep my hands off your abs.'

Maybe I should have cut her a little slack. It sounded like both of us were born with a touch of madness. I still couldn't believe how good she looked and how smiley and happy she was.

The teddy bear concerned me a little bit. I was sure there was a perfectly reasonable explanation for it, but all I could think of was that she had sacrificed it during some sort of weird witch experiment in an attempt to curse an ex-boyfriend.

We made our way to breakfast. I don't think it could have been more awkward. Her dad sat opposite me at the table, staring me out in silence the whole time while drinking his coffee. He obviously wanted to hurt me. Maybe even kill me. He wasn't blinking. Maybe we woke him up when we got in the night before. I had no idea. Also, I don't reckon wearing an undone suede shirt with his daughter's name scratched into my chest at the breakfast table helped my cause or the fact that his giddy daughter couldn't keep her hands off my arm the whole time.

He was a tall, good-looking, white Irish man. A scary-looking bloke with a weathered face. He had big hands and looked like he knew what to do with them. It wasn't until later that Mona told me that he worked for his notorious cousins, the O'Brien's. That wasn't a family to mess with. They pretty much ran the city's underworld. I kept my head down and tried to avoid his sinister gaze.

Her mother was from Morocco. It was easy to see where Mona got her looks from. She was beautiful, absolutely stunning, and looked more like a darker-skinned sister than her mum. Her time during breakfast was kept busy serving us pancakes, bacon and toast while making teas and coffees and trying to fill the silence with questions and stories to ease the awkward tension. Truth be told, she seemed a little excited by my surprise appearance.

There were no signs yet that her mother wasn't bat shit crazy, like Mona. However, I still felt uneasy whenever she picked up a knife. Maybe the psycho came from her dad. I looked up at him and caught his stare. Yeah, the psycho side definitely came from him. What a fucking lunatic. Why wasn't he blinking? He'd not even said a word, and I could already tell he were fucking mental. I don't think he broke his stare even to eat his breakfast.

I'd been boxing most of my life, and I worked out nearly every day. I knew how to handle myself, and I knew how to take a punch. I wasn't scared of anyone until I met Mona's dad.

He picked up a knife to butter his toast—bloody hell. I don't know how anyone could butter a bit of bread so aggressively. The knife went through the toast at one point. I had to get out of there.

After I had finished eating, I thanked her mum and dad for the breakfast and said that I'd better be getting off as I didn't want to disturb their weekend any further. Her mum offered me another cup of tea before I left, one for the road. That was the only time her dad broke his stare from me and instead turned to his wife with the same cutting glare to imply that she shouldn't have said that. I took the hint and insisted that I really ought to leave.

'I'll drive you home!' Mona yelled out with excitement.

She had a car. She had a car as well as being able to do that thing with her mouth. There was a Fleetwood Mac poster on her wall, and she looked like a supermodel…"

-

"Mona and I officially became an item just a few weeks after the night we met. She was the one who asked me to be her boyfriend—I wanted to, of course, but also, I was a little scared to say no, just in case she tried to stab me.

From then on, we were inseparable. She was still mental but in a sort of adorable way. We were with each other nearly every hour of the day; if I wasn't with Mo, that was, and if Mona wasn't studying or working at the cafe.

Katie was introduced to us through Mona. They went to university together. Mona and Katie hit it off in class during their first semester when Mona saw that Katie was wearing a Heart band T-shirt.

By the time summer came around, the four of us were a little gaggle of chaos. We were forever stoned in Mona's car, driving around the city, looking at life through a vintage lens where only rock and roll fantasies prevailed, like some sort of seventies pop group. Mo and Katie would be in the back of the car. Mo, rolling the spliffs and cracking jokes, while Katie would be singing and dancing along to the sound of the speakers.

I always thought that Katie looked like the blonde one from Abba and dressed a little like her, too. She was very nostalgically stylish, a fashionista, and a really pretty girl. She wasn't as pretty as Mona—no one was—but she was still exceptionally beautiful in her own right.

Mona and I would be in the front of the car, chain-smoking cigarettes and trying to keep our hands off each other. Often, Mona wore tiny little dresses that made her long, silky, bronze legs hard to resist.

Without a doubt, my girlfriend was borderline psychopathic, that never changed. And she was very excitable all the time too, that never changed either. We would fall out and make up, often over trivial things that were usually my fault. Mona was a very jealous person. We always made up quickly, but sometimes, she would go a little over the top with her insecurities and psychotic personality traits. I lost a few pairs of trainers and T-shirts to her rage.

Incidentally, we would have done nearly anything for each other. Apart from Mo, Mona was my best friend. We knew everything about the other and didn't keep any secrets.

I never spent the night around Mona's again. Her dad was too intense; he scared me more than she did. I went for a couple of awkward dinners, but that was it. Mona pretty much lived at my flat. We would eat together, shop together, and even work out together. It was incredible how good she looked in her gym gear, or any outfit, for that matter.

We'd stay up late, drinking and smoking weed, planning out our future together while listening to music from the last half-century. She loved rock and roll just as much as I did. Mona would even cut my hair for me. I didn't like it going in my eyes when I was boxing.

A spare key was made so she could let herself in after her classes while I was still at work at the call centre. I stopped working at Rex's bar just before I met Mona because I wanted a job during the day to free up my evenings and weekends to play in bands.

As mental as the stunner was, and she really was, I loved her a lot. We loved each other. We even got matching tattoos. It was her idea. Mine was on my ribs; hers was on the inside of her forearm. The tattoo was a Bruce Springsteen lyric. It said, 'This gun's for hire, even if we're just dancing in the dark'. We used to get really drunk and dance half-naked in the kitchen to that song.

Mona was an incredible artist. A painter. That's what she studied at university. She would paint in my flat. We would paint together. Then, I would put the pieces up on the wall. Her mysterious multi-coloured marine monster was one of my favourites. I would often think about the night that she painted it. Shirtless and braless, with The Doors playing in the background and a spliff hanging from her mouth. While it dried, we had sex on the floor of my living room. That was the night we said we'd be a forever kind of thing and would never break up. I meant it. We both did."

Chapter Five

"Jack, let me tell you about her family. Would you like a cigar? No? Okay.

In 2007, the same morning you woke up in your flat to all the cash, three aggressors who were born into a life of hostility, crime, and violence were sitting in their office. It was their city and their family who called the shots out on the streets and dominated the city's warfare through violence and corruption. Their organisation distributed the means of supplying the city with the narcotics of a nastier nature. Anything people wanted, they would sort. Cocaine, meth, MDMA, weed, heroin, pills, crack… anything. A family that was evil and sinister, undefeated and unmatched. The O'Brien's.

Officially, they were car dealers, but that was their only legal enterprise. It was a coverup for where the real money was made, drugs and violence.

Their car yard in Hardwick, Manchester, scaled the size of two football pitches. Inside was an array of cars. Some were new, some were old, and some were written off.

In the middle of the yard was their cabin office, which sat in front of three locked shipping containers that held some of the contents of their illegal activity—mainly drugs and money. The rest of their stock was spread across the city in different locations.

The yard's perimeter was completely fenced off, and closed-circuit television cameras covered each corner. There were only two ways in and out of the gangster's playground. The first was through the main entrance, on the roadside. That was gated and locked each night by the on-duty security guard, whose shift would be rotated among the many men who worked for them. The second was a secret gate hidden from the cameras around the back. That exit opened onto a smaller, muddy road, just big enough for a van to fit down without getting stuck. The route around the back circled the perimeter and ended up back on the main road. That was how they transported their contraband in and out of their property without being recorded by their security cameras, just in case the police came knocking for the tapes one day.

At the back of the yard, parallel to the main road, was a fenced-off and busy set of noisy train tracks that ran thousands of people in and out of the city all day, every day.

Commercial and industrial warehouses neighboured the yard. They, too, had small, overgrown, grassy roads running along the back, but only the O'Brien's frequented the route. Though I know you knew most of that.

Inside the unpainted and unwelcoming office sat three brothers.

Conor, the eldest. He was in his mid-thirties. A tall, white, handsome man with short, thick, dark hair and a pair of masculine slugs for eyebrows. Conor was strong-built and intellectually gifted. Calm and calculated. Although he was not the head of the family, he was an alpha male and a ferocious businessman.

A drunken and beautiful wife undercooked overpriced meals for him each night. They'd been an item since their school days and lived in a big house in the city with their three young children. Two boys and one girl. Patrick, Ashley and Kerry.

Conor's teachers thought wonders of him during his school years. He was always incredibly charming, witty, and bright and would often dazzle the room with charisma and intellect before beating some wrongdoer up behind the bike shed. His teachers encouraged him to continue his studies once he left school, but the family business was the only way he was headed.

As a teen, he would box and play football. He could have been a professional at either, but he didn't have a choice;

his dad had already carved out the path he had to walk his life down.

He had an exceptional knack for talking his way out of trouble, which helped him get out of a lot of sticky situations peacefully. Incidentally, he was no pushover, quite the opposite, with the potential to be a real horrible bastard when he needed to be. And he needed to be a lot in his line of work.

The bearded gangster had an ambitious eye for the future. Once his parents had died, he thought he would move the family towards legitimate business—or at least he hoped to.

As his boots rested on the surface of his busy and paperwork-cluttered desk, which was furthest away and diagonal to the door of the cabin office, he read the morning paper in silence while occasionally running his fingers through his short hair to try and aid the slight headache of a hangover. He was also trying to ignore the nonsensical comments from his stoned brothers.

The second brother, Liam, was Opposite Conor, supplying most of the comments.

Liam was two years younger, four inches taller, thirty kilograms heavier, and was nearly always in a tracksuit. Unlike his older brother, he was bald, clean-shaven and as ugly as sin with a hell of a beer belly. He'd spent a spell behind bars in his twenties for viciously beating a man.

Liam's ugly face had caught a few permanent war wounds throughout the years. He had a scar on his chin, his right cheek and below and above his right eye.

Four local murders all pointed towards him as the culprit, but there was no significant evidence to prove his guilt. Though everyone knew it was him.

During his time in prison, he made a lot of connections—good friends who became useful to the growth of the family business nationally. Not that they needed any help. The business had been booming since their dad started it in his twenties, not long after moving to the city.

Liam wasn't very bright at school and wasn't charming either—he was terrible with the ladies. His only skill in life was hand-to-hand combat. He was an incredible fighter—very quick, very strong, and very well-balanced. He coached down a boxing gym his cousin owned in the city a few days a week.

On his right index and middle fingers, he always wore two huge golden rings that had caved in the faces of many hardened men.

Nothing phased him. He never showed any signs of shock or remorse. He was a total psychopath, willing to inflict maximum pain for the smallest jabs of disrespect.

At his empty desk, he sat, smoking a cigarette and listening to the radio. He laughed loudly at the half-witted jokes the radio presenter made between records while sipping a mug of piping hot black coffee and occasionally glaring at his uninterested older brother.

To Liam's right was the third brother. He wasn't born an O'Brien, but he had been a member of the family since the age of ten. His name was Paddy Wang. The unofficially adopted youngest brother.

Paddy Wang had been best mates with Liam since the age of five when they met at primary school and bonded over a love of violence and arsonist interests.

Not long after Paddy Wang turned ten, he killed his parents in a house fire after a footballing disagreement during the Manchester derby. No one knew that it was him that started the fire, and there had been no suggestion ever of foul play.

The O'Brien's took him in and brought him up as one of their own. His nickname was born in a pub one Sunday afternoon when he was twelve. Paddy, after Big Paddy, the father of the O'Brien family, and Wang, which was the actual surname assigned to him at birth.

Paddy Wang was a very short and skinny-looking man of Chinese heritage who had a strong opinion on anything and everything and was incredibly unimpressed by all matters.

He always wore a perfectly ironed shirt and black trousers and loved suit shoes. He had many different styles and pairs, all incredibly expensive. On that day, he wore a pair of black leather Chelsea boots with a huge heel in a pathetic attempt to make him look taller.

A black lion-headed cane was constantly carried in his hand, which he would often use as either a weapon or a way to implement his opinion by striking various surfaces to prominently signify his thoughts in such a way that needed no translation.

An immaculately trimmed thin moustache sat above the little angry-looking man's top lip, and his slick and wet-looking side parted combed over hair never moved a strand out of position.

Chiselled in glory, the little man would do twenty consecutive muscle-ups as a warmup each day before he began his workout. He was incredibly competent at a mix of martial arts, such as Brazilian ju-jitsu, karate, and boxing.

He and Liam shared an apartment in the city centre that was more like a conveyer belt for drugs, hookers and card games.

Paddy Wang sat with his chair facing out of the window, smoking a spliff and observing the summer sky in deep and captivated thought. His desk was closest to the door but far enough away to not be interrupted by the motion of the opening and closing. It was perfectly organised with piles of books, paperwork and quality golden-plated ornaments such as an ashtray, a miniature mantel clock and a miniature globe.

There were four desks with four expensive reclinable swivel chairs in the office that were all positioned so that the owner of each faced inwards. A different coloured ashtray sat in the corner of them all, with the same golden Zippo lighter to the side, engraved with the name *O'Brien*—three for the brothers and the fourth for their dad, Big Paddy.

Big Paddy's workspace sat Opposite Paddy Wang's and was the only desk with a computer and a landline telephone on it. The surface was loaded with legitimate paperwork and financial records that Conor and Paddy Wang would sift through for a couple of hours a week to keep their car dealership in working and legal order. Behind the desk hung a car calendar that was bare from appointments and a framed vintage Irish football shirt.

The office radio was positioned on a metal-legged table against the back wall to Liam's left. It had on it a coffee machine, a selection of different mugs and a couple of bottles of Irish whiskey. Above the table hung a framed Manchester City home shirt from 1995 and a basic analogue clock. Beneath the table was a bin and a mini fridge with only milk and beer in it. A folded chair neatly rested beside it. Next to the table, by Connor's desk, was a back door that led to the toilet.

Paddy Wang watched as a black Range Rover drove through the yard and pulled up close to the cabin to park. Moments later, the office door flew open, and a pair of unexpected but very welcome visitors walked in. A giant, bald man who took a seat behind the unused desk and an exceptionally beautiful, well-dressed lady. Both were in their sixties.

The woman walked up to Paddy Wang gracefully and took his spliff from him. She then smiled maternally and began to smoke it, taking in big drags as she did. Paddy Wang swivelled around and got to his feet so that the woman could sit comfortably in his chair. She stroked him on the shoulder, with love in her eyes, and then sat and observed the other two men in the room, who hadn't yet acknowledged the new arrivals.

Her name was Alannah. She was a very classy and well-dressed white brunette who moved over from Ireland in her twenties, the same time Big Paddy and his cousins did. They were only a couple of years apart in age, Alannah the younger. She was his one true love and the only one who could get through to him in the moments of madness.

Everything about her was expensively maintained, from her hair to her nails. She would always be wearing the finest jewellery in the room, no matter the room.

The big man sat down and typed away on the computer's keyboard, looking intently as he did so with a slight squint that suggested he needed glasses but was too proud to admit it.

Paddy wang had walked over to the foldable chair tucked away neatly next to the fridge and sat in the corner of the room by Liam's desk. He was smoking a cigarette that he had taken from his brother's pack while observing the dissatisfaction on his mother's face from still having not received a welcome from her other sons.

The big man read the computer screen for a moment, analysing in depth the figures of his endeavours. He then turned his head right to look at his eldest son. In disgust, deep creases of anger showed on his weathered face as he glared in silence at the newspaper reading Heir of Anarchy.

Paddy O'Brien. Big Paddy, the leader of notorious business affairs, climbed to the top to become the city's most feared criminal. He incited violence and theft in the shadows of the city's underworld. Ferociously, he became a big-time drug dealer who made a lot of money in a short amount of time and got greedy. He was never caught; he never could have been, as he was always clever enough to ensure there was never any evidence that could lead to a trial.

The god-forsaken gangster made a lot of friends around the city, and they all worked together towards the same objective, with him as their leader. Each had their own legitimate businesses to cover their illegalities. Big Paddy had the car dealership. One mate, Stephen, had a pub in Rusholme. Another mate, Chris, owned a gym in Salford, and his cousin, Aidan, owned a garage in Salford. Others were nightclub owners, bouncers, barber shop owners, landlords, bookies, lawyers and estate agents. Even a few bent policemen were acquaintances and on his books.

Big Paddy had a huge belly and massive arms the size of a normal man's legs. He must have weighed around a hundred and thirty kilograms, maybe more. He was a tall man, but not as tall as Liam. His knuckles were heavily callused from bare-knuckle boxing, and his monstrous face was ugly and looked ten years older than it was.

Eternally without peace, his anger was short-fused, and the velocity of his rage was without shame. The villainous racketeer was relentlessly addicted to the darkness, to the madness and the maintenance of his vampiric reputation. Even though he had taken a back seat over the past few years and didn't do any of the dirty work physically himself, he still enjoyed nothing more than beating a man to a pulp.

The big, tattooed bruiser spent most of his days reclused on his farm on the city's outskirts. He had acres of land with a fancy house built in the heart of it. It was a fully working farm, with livestock and agriculture, not much, but it was enough to keep him busy. A few chickens, some pigs and some sheep. He never enjoyed the farm life and pretended he had more of an idea of what was going on and how it all worked than he really did. He just liked killing the animals.

You wouldn't have guessed that Big Paddy was a multi-millionaire by looking at him. His clothes were very expensive, but you'd never have known. He wore the uniform of a football casual. A hooligan that was reluctant of peacocking, choosing dark and simple shades. He often wore a black polo shirt, a black Harrington jacket, dark blue jeans, and a pair of black suede Adidas trainers. The flashiest of statements he ever made were in his golden Rolex wristwatches and his supercar collection, though the cars were also vacant of colour.

'Did ya deal with it?' Big Paddy asked his son. His bellowing Irish accent was as strong as ever.

'We did.' Conor replied in a deep Mancunian tone without looking up from his newspaper.

'Did ya get any grief from your man?'

'None at all, Dad.'

Then Paddy Wang slapped his cane onto Liam's desk aggressively and scowled at his eldest brother.

'Alright… We had a little trouble, but it was nothing our Liam couldn't handle without it getting silly. All of it was there. Their man lost a tooth for getting a bit mouthy about our little brother, and I don't think his pal will be walking right for a while. It's all in the lock-up. Shane's in there now, cutting it up. Then he and Tom will be dropping it off to the boys later.' that was all said, still without lifting his head from the newspaper.

'You know t score, Son. Accepting disrespect is t damnation of your honour. You turn a blind eye t one wrongdoing, and soon, t devil's work will be done for ya. You strike and have it be done now. Send Hector round t finish your man off properly. Have him break both his kneecaps. Ten drive him ten miles out of town and tell him t walk back. Your man will be hell-bound in no time, and our great reputation will be free from harm.' A small and bellowing chuckle came from Liam on the other side of the room at his dad's words. Liam was staring at the ceiling while leaning back on his chair and smoking his lungs into oblivion. Paddy Wang removed his cane from the desk and curved a sinister half smile. Conor lifted his head from his paper and turned to look at his dad.

'Hector is on the way round, but not to fucking kill him.

He's just going to rough him up a bit and tax him a one-er. He's taking Billy with him. If we keep killing everyone over the smallest of sins, then people will be too scared to do business with us, and they'll start selling to our competitors. And then there'll be a fucking war. We need their fear, but more importantly, we need their money. Also, we don't want any more people going missing this year. We couldn't deal with it properly at the time, not with all that gear in the back of the car. We needed to be in and out, and it took twenty seconds too long for my liking, breaking the bastard's leg. He will be dealt with Dad. Our reputation won't be harmed.'

Big Paddy stared at Conor without emotion, trying not to reveal his irritation. Big Paddy knew that he and his other sons would have handled it differently. It would have ended in murder. The eldest son was more calculated, which would eventually lead to a brighter future for the family's business. Big Paddy half knew that but refused to fully admit it to himself.

Alannah rose gracefully from her chair and walked over to Liam's desk. She handed Paddy Wang back his spliff and stroked Liam's cheek before turning the radio off to address the room in a thick Irish accent.

'And what about t money tat went missing last night?'

The three brothers looked at each other, trying to hide their shock. That had caught their attention fully.

'How did you hear about that?' Liam asked in a deep grunt while pulling another cigarette from the packet on his desk. Conor put his paper down, removed his legs from the top of his desk, and then pulled open a drawer from below to retrieve his cigarettes. While lighting one, his father spoke to the room.

'You tort we didn't know about tat. Ay? And, from t look on ya faces, it looks like you weren't planning on telling us about it any time soon. Well, never mind how we know; just know tat we do know. You boys don't seem to have an inkling of who your man is yet, either, do you? Just how much did tis fucker get away with last night?'

'Just over four grand.' Conor replied while exhaling smoke.

There was a silence. Everyone's eyes shifted from Conor, and they were firmly focused on Big Paddy, awaiting his orders. The anticipation grew to become almost tangible. No one had ever dared to steal that much money from the family before, and the ones who had tried stealing smaller amounts met their maker not long after.

After a moment's pause and contemplation, the big man began.

'Ahh, four grand is fuck all. I've pissed tat much tis morning and have made it twice back already. It's not even fucking lunch money lads. But, as you know, tat's not the fucking point! Fucking no, it is fucking not! We will get tat money back. Find your man tat stole it and deal with him. Properly. No messing about. I want his head on a fucking stake. You hear me!? It's about principle. It's about honour. It's about respect! Any fucker who dares steal from us will pay the ugly price. I want t know who he is, and I want to know where his family is! How did your man get hold of t money anyway? Who fucked up!?'

Conor turned his head to look at his brothers and then turned back to face his dad, exhaling smoke and flirting with the idea to try and cover up his ignorance of the technicalities of the theft. He pondered for a moment before nodding to Liam to tell the room what happened.

Liam took a big drag of his cigarette and then began in an even deeper and bellowing Mancunian accent than his brother's.

'Well… I went to pick the money up from Craig. He was throwing a bit of a party round his gaff. Few people, nothing special. The money was all there, in a bag in the kitchen. There was this geezer running about the place. A young lad. Off his fucking nut. No one had a fucking clue who he was, who he came with or why he was there. He didn't have a fucking clue who we were, either. That pissed me off. Anyway, I stayed for a beer, and this lad got kicked out the place not long after. He nearly got a good hiding, too, but he looked like he'd already had a bit of trouble, so Craig left it alone. Looked like he'd be roughed up to fuck. Proper. You know, face and hands were bloodied up. Couldn't really make out what he looked like. T-shirt was all ripped. I still reckon he shoulda cut him. Not long after he was kicked out, we noticed that just over four grand was missing from the bag, but it was too late; he were gone. We sent a few of the boys out on a search for him but there was no luck. We couldn't find him. He just disappeared into the night.'

Big Paddy was fuming. His face had turned to a shade of red. It looked like his head was about to burst as the thick veins in his neck became big enough to get a coach down. He pulled out a cigarette and lit it with his golden zippo. Then he took a drag so big that it burned through over half the length of it.

'Tis is not fucking good, boys! Not good at all! We need t find out who your man is and get tat money back. Quick time, too! T fucking cheek of it. Liam and Paddy, you two, get round a few a places and do some asking about, see what anybody knows about your man. Find him. But be discrete! T less people tat know t details, t better. Conor, drive your mother home, and ten make sure your men have everything tey need for tonight. We can't be having any more fuck ups. None! Tese lads can't be running dry. It's Saturday, t city will be bouncing. A lot of money t be made. After you've done tat, link up with your brothers and try and find your man from last night. Someone must know something. Find him! I want his fucking head! Don't none of you's come back here later on either. I'm meeting Cousin Ronan and his man McDonald in a few hours for a game of cards and t settle a bit of business. We'll be here for t night. I don't want t be fucking disturbed. Is tat fucking understood? And lads, you better sort tis fucking mess. Do I make myself clear?'

There was a murmur around the room, and each of the sons acknowledged their father's demands without any eye contact, like embarrassed schoolchildren being told off by the headmaster. Then they all got to their feet and left the office to do their duty, all emotion drained from their faces.

Alannah scowled at her husband as she stormed out first, showing exaggerated frustrations at her husband for attending to business on a Saturday night. A night that was usually devoted to her.

Conor was the last to leave. He turned to nod at his dad before he left. A gesture that was only met with a gaze of serious resentment."

Chapter Six

Jack turned away from the cigar-smoking man and looked at the fire. He was anxious to relive what came next. It was a memory he hid from. He knew he would never forget it, even if he wanted to.

"It was that summer night in 2007.

Mo and I waited until the cover of darkness to put his plan into action. I couldn't help but wonder whether the idea was either genius or completely fucking stupid.

We'd been back to my flat, tidied up a bit and hidden the money from the night before in a gym bag behind the sofa. I managed to clean some of the blood off the money by rubbing the notes with anti-bacterial wipes.

While Mo got high and listened to my Red Hot Chilli Peppers CD, I showered again, for the second time that day, and dressed in black, ready for the night ahead: black jeans, a plain black jumper, and my black Converse. I lent Mo a black zip-up hoodie. His multi-coloured shirt wouldn't have complimented the theme of being hidden in the shadows while being one with the night.

Then, just like all the greatest military operations, the public bus was our mode of transport…

Once off the bus, the streetlights guided us down an eroded pavement. On either side, overgrown grass grew through the cracks of the city's forgotten streets, miles away from all hope and opportunity. The further we got, the fewer people and cars there were as the domestic world morphed into rundown commercial business parks, barren from life and event, and not only because of the hour.

There wasn't a cloud in the night sky. The stars danced nakedly, flickering and watching us, more than likely mocking us if they knew our ambition.

I was smoking a cigarette, and Mo was smoking a spliff that we were passing back and forth between us.

The hippy's hood was up, and his middle-parted hair was neatly tucked behind his ears, with the sides hanging out the front of his hood like a scarf. His rose-tinted glasses were on the top of his nose. I often wondered how he managed to find his way through the night with them on. He was also wearing a black backpack with the tools we needed for the job inside it.

We both knew the plan. A different gear had clicked within us since we stepped off the bus into Hardwick, though the weed was making me feel a little apprehensive.

'Do you think there'll be any dogs, man?' Mo asked quietly.

'Fuck sake. Why have you only thought this now? Did Micky not say anything about dogs?'

'My dude. It was years ago that I spoke to him about this place. And we were really fucked up that night, man, like really fucked up. Mad pills and vodka, dude. He told me where the cameras face and about the secret gate around the back. He might have said something about a dog... or maybe there was just a dog in the pub that night... or... I don't know, man.' Mo admitted while handing me the smoke.

'Jesus. You're dealing with them if they come running.' Mo laughed.

'Jack, what if they have ten dogs?' We both laughed harder, trying to keep the noise down as we creased up, which made it even harder to stop laughing. We were probably too stoned for a trip to the supermarket, let alone an ambitious attempt at grand theft auto.

We walked in silence for a few more minutes down the commercial roads. Warehouses filled the scene from left to right. There wasn't a soul in sight, and hadn't been for a while.

'Fuck. Look. There it is.' Mo whispered. He was right. I could see it. About three hundred meters away, on the left side of the road. The O'Brien's yard. It looked shitter than I had expected. There was a large, basic rundown sign by the entrance that just said *O'Brien Motors* on a plain white board in a salient black font.

We stopped and took a step to the side of the path. We were up close to the walls of a warehouse, hiding in the shadows and smoking while quietly going over the plan one final time.

'What if we fuck it up? What about the security guard?' I asked quietly.

'We'll be fine, man. Have a little faith. Stick to the plan.' He knew I felt uneasy. Then Mo slid off the rucksack from his back and pulled out a hip flask.

'What's in that?' I asked.

'A little liquid luck, my dude.' Mo took a swig and then handed it to me. It was whiskey. I took two swigs and instantly felt a lot better, though I still had a bad feeling about it all.

After finishing the spliff, we turned back to walk away from the yard. We reached a grassy side road two warehouses away from the O'Brien's. That was our access, the muddy off-road that ran along the train tracks behind the O'Brien's place—the one you were talking about. Our plan was to go in through the back. That would give us better coverage and a longer time away from civilian sight to remove suspicion. Not that there was anybody around to see us.

It was pitch black down the side of the warehouse. With each step, my breath was held so long that I almost forgot to breathe. I was too stoned. We had to tread carefully by testing with a hovering feel before fully planting our foot down to advance. It took a lot longer than I had expected it to, or maybe that was just the weed.

Mo led the way. The sound of train travel going into and out of the city nearly every other minute had been audible since we'd gotten off the bus, but down the side road, it became near deafening as we got closer to the tracks. The only light that passed was from the carriage windows, illuminating just enough to see Mo's silhouette in front of me.

At the end of the side road, we turned right to pass along the back of the two neighbouring warehouses. Each step felt like a trigger, abusing a game of Russian roulette. We were slow and cautious, sweating from the anticipation. The smell of the summer night mixed with overgrown grass and the rusted metallics of train travel were almost thick enough to touch. The passing trains softly blew a reminder of reality onto our skin. I had a doubtful intuition, and it grew more aggressively with each step. My legs were ready to run as I lost control of my thoughts, overthinking all the possible ways the plan could turn to disaster.

After what seemed like an eternity, finally, there it was, lit up in all its glory by sporadic flood lights. The O'Brien's yard. There must have been nearly one hundred cars in there. They were everywhere. Different shapes and sizes. All parked neatly in rows with an unmarked system that navigated a route around the place.

We crept along the railway fence, staying as tight as we could while using the shadows as cover and staying still whenever a train went by so that our position wasn't compromised in the passing light by any possible onlooking eyes.

After about fifteen minutes, we reached the yard's back gate. It was double-doored and chained together from the middle, hinged to open inwards towards the yard.

We stood for a few minutes, observing and listening for signs of life. We couldn't see the office; it was hidden behind the shipping containers around fifty meters away. We couldn't see any dogs either. I thought maybe that was just a myth, or they were sleeping by the office. Both were positive signs, at least.

We could, however, hear men laughing from inside the office, with music playing. It was very faint, but if we concentrated in the moments when no trains were passing, we could just about hear it. We had anticipated that there would be at least one security guard; that much was common knowledge, but we were less prepared to deal with more.

Mo knelt and took his backpack off. I knelt with him. He pulled out a cordless angle grinder from inside the bag and handed it to me. He then zipped his bag closed and secured the straps safely through his arms so that it rested again on his back.

I knew the plan. I waited until the next train passed, rose, and pressed forward towards the gate. Using the light and sound of the train as cover, I began sawing through the chain sealed by the padlock. Sparks of light flew out as I cut through the metal. It was in our favour that the security cameras couldn't see that part of the yard.

The train had passed before I'd managed to cut all the way through. I released the pressure from the trigger. I would have to wait for the next train to pass before the job could be finished. Just one more push and we would have been in. It would have taken no more than five additional seconds. There was only a millimetre or so left to get through. It looked as if it could snap clean off by itself at any moment as it hung there with the weighted lock pulling it down.

I heard the ignition of a lighter over my left shoulder. Mo had lit a cigarette. What was he thinking? Then, the sound of two dogs barking came from behind the shipping containers. They had heard Mo light his smoke and were trying to direct the men in the office towards our compromised position.

Mo and I moved quickly to either side of the gate, where we lay prone, hidden in the shadows."

"Jack, let me tell you something quick.
Inside the office that night, Big Paddy, his cousin Ronan

and a man named McDonald were all receiving lap dances around Liam's desk from half-dressed, drugged-up young women. The card game he had told his family about had become a seedy little party. The hookers hadn't arrived there too long before, as the women hadn't endured any of the men sexually. Playing cards were still set up, faced down around Liam's desk with piles of cash and used ashtrays next to them. More cash and a plate of cocaine was in the middle of the table, that everyone in the room had taken a lot of. Bottles of empty beer were all around that end of the room, too, and the radio at the back of the office was playing hits from the eighties.

Big Paddy ordered Ronan to go and have a look at what the dogs were barking at. Ronan reluctantly removed the dancing prostitute from his lap and went outside to check.

The still barking chained-up dogs were facing the direction of the back gate, though they couldn't see you as the shipping containers were in the way. The eighties music got louder, as you know, and then the office door closed.

Ronan walked around to the side of the containers and stood observing the gate from a distance. After a minute, he decided whatever the dogs were barking at was not a cause for concern. He thought it was likely nothing. No one had ever tried to break into the yard before, and he was eager for another line of coke and to get back to his lap dance. So he joined the party back inside the office, handing everyone in the room a beer before sitting back down to enjoy the young woman again.

Big Paddy's prostitute was bent over Liam's table, doing a line of cocaine, trying to hide the hurt she felt from the big handprint on her naked bum cheek from when Big Paddy had spanked her a little too hard moments before. She'd not had the chance to finish the full length of her line; Big Paddy had aggressively pulled her by the hair back to his chair to continue with the dance while he drank his beer and rubbed his dirty hand over her naked breast."

"Bloody hell…

Mo and I waited ten minutes before attempting to break into the yard again. I signalled to Mo that I would finish the cutting the next time a train went past.

Two minutes later, I was back at it. A train was passing, and sparks were flying everywhere in front of me. It took a matter of seconds before I'd cut all the way through.

Still covered by the sound of the train, Mo unravelled the chains to free the gate and then pushed his side open—a little too hard. As the sound of the train disappeared, the creaking of the gate opening continued, setting the dogs off barking again.

We jumped down, back in the prone on either side of the double-doored gate, panicking and full of rioting butterflies in our stomachs. Half the gate was fully open, and there was no time to close it before we heard the office door open for a second time. The sound of the music again grew louder for the duration of the time that the door was open. The door closed. My heart lay in my throat, beating at speeds I didn't know a body could allow.

Ronan was back outside to see what the dogs were barking at. He walked to the side of the shipping containers to observe the back gate, just like he had before. That time, he could see why the dogs were so excited.

The mobster pulled out a pistol that was tucked into the back of his trousers. He cocked it and made the weapon ready. Then he slowly walked forward towards the open gate. With each step, my courage wore thinner as the sound of his heavy boots got closer and closer. Ronan couldn't see us. We were hidden in the dark. I could only see his silhouette as he made his way to the back of the yard. Something about him looked familiar. Maybe it was his walk. I couldn't work out what it was, but I was sure that I knew him.

The Irish gangster got close to the gate; his gun was

pointed at the ready, prepared to inflict maximum violence towards whoever was lurking in the darkness. I knew he couldn't see us, though I was almost frightened that the intensity of my beating heart would give our position away.

Mo wasn't looking. His head was buried into the ground and had been since the pistol was revealed.

Ronan got to the gate and looked to his right. He stared intently at Mo, certain that someone was lying on the ground. If it wasn't for Mo's trainers, he might not have seen him.

He slowly pointed his gun in Mo's direction. My heart was at the back of my tongue. I had to act quickly. He was about to shoot. I was panicking and didn't have time to think anything through with logic.

I pounced up and hit him around the head with the angle grinder before he had the chance to fire his weapon. I hit him hard. It rocked him, and he took a stumbled step backwards. I'd caught him by surprise and was terrified that he would shoot us both once he'd gathered his bearings. So I hit him again, harder, and in the same spot as before.

Ronan dropped his gun and then fell and hit the back of his head hard on the ground. We never heard him hit the concrete; a passing train masked the thud of his collapse. Blood began to pour out of his skull. I took a cautious step forward. It was when I saw him lying down that the floodlights revealed his face. I'd really fucked up. Fucking hell… It was Mona's dad…

Mo got to his feet. We both stood over the dying body, staring at him. Wide-eyed and disoriented.

'Fuck, man. Should we get him some aspirin? I've got some with me.' Mo suggested as blood poured out from Ronan's skull, trying to make light of and not accept the severity of the crime that I'd just committed. There was so much blood.

'Mate… That's Mona's dad.' I replied in a low and

sombre tone. I was in immense shock and was struggling to believe and accept what I'd done. Being stoned wasn't helping at all. Mo could barely contain himself.

'What?... What the fuck? Are you sure? No way. Like, are you one hundred per cent? It can't be. Why would Mona's dad be here?' he whispered frantically.

'You know Mona's surname, right?' I asked him.

'No?'

'It's O'Brien. Her names Mona O'Brien. Her dad's, Big Paddy's cousin. He works for them.'

Mo couldn't hide how troubled he was to learn the news. His hands rubbed the hair under his hoodie as he turned away to try and process what I had just said.

'Fuck off, man. Fucking hell… Jack?! Why the fuck didn't you tell me this before? Why did we come here if she's one of them?' Mo whispered assertively. He was panicking. We both were, but I was too frozen to move.

'They're not close. She doesn't speak to any of them. She says Big Paddy's a creep. He was always too hands-on with her at family parties, so she stopped going. Fuck. Fucking hell. This is bad, man. This is really fucking bad.' My hands, my back and my forehead were sweating profusely. It was hot, really hot. I thought I was going to throw up as my heart continued to beat on overdrive. I stood there, shivering like a tree in a storm. I didn't know what to do. Should we have run away? I was used to fucking up, but even I had never fucked up that badly before.

The dogs were still barking. They could smell that something was wrong. I'd never seen that much blood before. A gigantic puddle had formed around his head as he lay there, open-eyed, looking just as hostile as he did when he was alive. He looked evil, like a man who hadn't met his peace in the afterlife. There was no doubt that he was dead.

'My dude, we need to go now, or we're going the same fucking way. Quick, grab a leg.' Mo instructed.

Mo picked up Ronan's gun and tucked it down the back of his waistband. I dropped the angle grinder, and we grabbed a leg each and dragged him a few meters out of the way of the gate. Blood smeared from where he had fallen. It left a huge red trail of murder.

Then I opened my side of the gate so that a car could fit through and we could escape in a stolen vehicle.

I picked up the angle grinder back up and looked at it for a moment. Around twenty-four hours before I was sitting in a bar, I didn't have thousands of pounds of stolen cash behind my sofa, I didn't owe Ricky a new car, and I hadn't killed my girlfriend's dad while trying to steal a car from the most notorious gangsters in the city.

Mo had already picked a motor. We had no time to be fussy. He was standing by the driver's door of a black BMW 3 Series, fifteen meters or so away from me. I ran over and found him completely duct-taping the driver's window so that you couldn't see any glass.

'What the fuck are you doing?' I asked in an aggressive whisper.

'If I duct tape it before smashing it, I'm less likely to get glass everywhere, and it should break in fewer cracks rather than shattering to shit.' Mo replied, looking like I should be impressed.

I reached down and tried the handle.

'It's unlocked, you dickhead.' I managed to tell him just in time before he smashed the window with a hammer. Mo looked pissed off that he didn't get to go through with his window-smashing plan—I was certain it wouldn't have worked as he imagined anyway.

He quickly put his tools back in the bag, and we both got in. The interior was pungent. It hit us with the smell of cigarettes and alcohol as soon as the door opened. I'd never smelled anything so bad. Incidentally, we didn't have the time to try another. We had to get the fuck out of the yard as quickly as possible. It was a good motor, too, and that was all Rex specified. He didn't say anything about the smell.

Mo was sat in the driver's seat, reaching around in his bag again. I was in the passenger side, lighting a cigarette to try and calm myself down. The distress I felt from murdering Mona's dad was something I couldn't compare to any emotion that I'd known before. I still felt sick and was drenched in buckets of sweat. I couldn't concentrate. The world began spinning around me as my knees shook.

Then Mo pulled a screwdriver out of the bag and leaned down.

'What the fucks that for?' I asked.

'I'm gonna hot wire it.' the hippy replied in a tone of competence before ducking his head beneath the dashboard. Mo really had thought of everything, apart from the fucking dogs.

Suddenly, I was dragged out of the car by my neck and was being choked out on the ground of the yard. I couldn't see who was doing it. My hands couldn't break free from the grip, nor could I breathe. My neck felt like it was about to crumble in the person's hands, like it was about to burst in their fingers. I had never felt a grip so strong. My eyes bulged, and my nose began to bleed. I was dying, and I knew it. Struggle after struggle, I tried to escape, but I was too weak against their will, desperately kicking my legs and trying to pull the giant hands off me. It was no use; the strangler was too strong. My closed eyes were seeing stars, and all the sound began to disappear. My oxygen was being starved further by my panic. I couldn't control my fear. My head felt light, and my effort to survive was at the cusp of defeat. I was close to death and knew that I had only seconds left.

Then I heard a gunshot. The grip around my neck loosened. I lay there choking in agonising pain while trying to get my breath back. The stars in my vision slowly faded as the colour of the world returned. My ears rang a singular note of white noise that got quieter and quieter as the seconds rolled on.

On top of me, the whale of a person who tried to kill me lay bleeding. Their warm blood began to trickle onto my shoulder. If I hadn't been in such a desperate position, I might have winced at the feel of it running down my skin.

I tried to push my attacker. It wouldn't work. He weighed too much and was slowly crushing me. Again, I tried, but the man wouldn't budge.

With a deep breath and a huge effort, I pushed and rolled the big man off me. I looked up to the night sky. Mo was standing there, pointing the gun at us both like a shaking statue in an earthquake.

My breath was back. I got to my feet and looked down at the man on the floor. It was Big Paddy.

We stared at the big man's dying body for a moment. His eyes seemed to be unable to close as he tried to hold pressure onto the gun wound leaking from his neck. Blood was pouring out. He was unable to talk. The choking began as he spewed out blood from his mouth, and his chest began to jerk.

'We need to fucking go, now!' I said with a sense of urgency, but Mo wasn't listening.

'Mo. We need to fucking go right now! Get in the car!' Mo snapped out of his trance. He looked at the gun in his hand and then looked at me.

'Mo!' I cried once more.

The hippy sprang into action and jumped back into the driver's seat. He began hotwiring the car. It wouldn't work. He kept trying. It wouldn't work. I got in, lit another cigarette and locked my door. My neck was in agony, and I couldn't work out if the blood on my hands was my own or Big Paddy's.

The car engine started. Mo let out a sigh of relief and passed me his bag. He shut his car door, and we drove off through the back fence, around the yard and onto the main road.

I undid my window slightly to let the smoke out. My mind was racing at a million miles an hour. I couldn't comprehend what had just happened...

Not much was said during the drive back to the city centre. I smoked half the cigarette before handing the second half to Mo. I then lit another and smoked in silence while trying to process the last half hour.

We drove through the city lights, passing hundreds of lairy lads and lasses. They were all provocatively intoxicated, attacking the night with dance and laughter while sharing a common ambition not to go home alone. In their gaggles, they sang the soundtrack to their vitality while oblivious to the care where sobriety resides in a way that only youth can truly tackle.

That is what Mo should have been doing. He should have been out that night until the early hours. Carefree and dancing. It's what we both should have been doing.

We went past Piccadilly Gardens and towards the Northern Quarter. The culture had changed in the past mile. A different community danced among those dancefloors. The girls had replaced their miniskirts with flares. The boys were less groomed and hairier. And the four-on-the-floor dance music had become suave and spicy rock and roll.

Mo turned and drove down a back road that the fire exit for Rex's bar was on. The burned-out car was still there. We parked behind it, and Mo called Rex to tell him to come outside.

Mo had already started rolling a spliff. He lit it and took four massive hits before handing it to me. Then he got out of the car to take the duct tape off the driver-side window.

I unlocked my door and joined Mo outside. His face was dejected as he peeled away the black tape and curled it into a ball. I handed Mo the spliff back and pulled out a cigarette. We were both silent and in our own heads.

Unable to stop replying, repeatedly, what had just happened in the yard. Mo wasn't a violent man. He'd never hurt a fly, though he and I would end the night as killers.

The back door of the bar flew open. John instantly sparked up a cigarette.

'Where the fuck did you two perverts get that from?' Rex asked aggressively. Mo and I stayed quiet.

Rex then slowly circled the car, intently observing.

'Who've you robbed that from?' John asked while exhaling smoke.

'It's not stolen.' I replied.

'Don't lie, knobhead.' said John, unamused at my blatant dishonesty.

'Alright, Mo? You little pervert.'

'Rex.' Mo replied glumly with a half nod. Rex opened the driver's door and had a look inside.

'Fucking hell. The smell of that.' Rex moaned.

Mo handed me the spliff. His hand was shaking as he did so, terrified that they would learn who we had stolen the car from, and then they would be able to link us with the deaths. It would only be a matter of hours before the news circled that the city's notorious kingpin had been murdered. I was more concerned with Mona and her finding out about her dad. I still hadn't turned my phone back on. Even before she learned about her dad, I knew I would be in trouble for not talking to her all day.

The night got worse. Rex closed the car's front door and opened the back. He peered in, examining with care. I couldn't work out his expression. A glimmer of shock was upon his poker face that even he couldn't hide.

'Who the fuck is that?' Rex asked.

I looked at Mo. What was he talking about? Rex looked up at me with an indignant resentment.

He asked again.

'Well? You little pervert. Who the fuck is it?'

I walked around to the opposite side of the car and opened the back door. Through the back window, I couldn't see anything. The darkness of the night wouldn't allow me to. Though, when the door was open, I could see it clearly. It was the shape of a man lying face up on the floor in front of the back seats. He looked to be in his late forties. A scruffy looker, unshaven and unclean. And he didn't look to be breathing either.

'Oi, mate.' Rex shouted at him to try and get him to wake up. John was at Rex's side, also glaring in.

Rex asked Mo to grab him an empty bottle of beer from an overflowing wheelie bin not far from where we stood. Rex was cautious; he knew it wouldn't be clever for his DNA to be found on the dead. So, he leant in and poked the man on the chest with the bottle repeatedly, trying to wake him.

'Oi! Pervert!' he said again while continuing to poke.

'Why the fuck have you brought him here?' Rex asked. His head was out of the car. He handed the bottle to John, and they swapped places. With a cigarette in his mouth, John leant in and began observing the body.

'He's dead, Boss.' John proclaimed while lifting his head out of the vehicle.

Rex stared at me, venom in his eyes, and then turned to Mo, who was standing by the bonnet.

'Well? What the fucks going on? Why the fuck have you brought me some dead geezer? Some sort of fucking joke? Think ya fucking funny? You two wanna fucking join him?!' the gang leader growled.

'Rex. Mate. We didn't know he was in there. Promise. We brought you this car in good faith. We didn't even check in the back, man.' I replied, scared as shit, while Mo's shaking hand lit another cigarette.

'Think I'm stupid? Think I'm some sort of fucking dickhead, do ya? I know exactly where you pair of pricks got this motor from. Fucking hell. Tryna start a fucking war, are ya? Going up against the fucking big boys? Ay? Christ alive. You thick fucks. This car has O'Brien practically written all over it. God fucking help you if they find out it were you… Jesus. Ferocious winds will cut through you like a storm you've never sailed, and you better have a jacket because your boat's got a great big fuck off hole in the bottom. You are gonna get wet, mate…

On the contrary, fair fucking dos. I like the style in which you perverts play. All is fair in love and car thievery. I admire your bottle. Intrepidity… I'll take the car. Ricky doesn't need to know the details. I'll sort the reg plates and all that shit—the legalities. You though, you little knobheads, you're gonna get rid of that geezer in the back. And fucking quick too. Drive him off, and then fuck him off. I don't wanna know where. I couldn't give a monkeys. Just get rid of him. Then get back here and give that car a good clean. The smell is borderline offensive. Make sure this is done by morning; we don't have time to mess about. And boys… not a word about this to anyone. Alright? No one. Now, fuck off… Go on.' said Rex.

I nodded at Rex's fear-striking gaze, struggling to process what had happened. There wasn't time to think about it. There wasn't even time to panic. We knew what we had to do. His instructions were clear, and he was going to sort it for us as long as we got rid of the body.

Mo and I jumped back into the car and drove off again into the heart of the city. Rex and John stood with an unbroken glare reflected in the car's mirrors.

We went past Piccadilly Station and down a quiet side road to formulate a plan. We needed to get away from onlooking eyes. Mo pulled over by the side of the road down a back street.

'Reach into the bag, dude, and pull out a couple cans.' Mo said. I pulled out two cans of lager from the rucksack. I handed one to Mo, and we drank them as quickly as we could. The alcohol helped us deal with the intensity of the past hour. It numbed us from emotion slightly and gave us the courage for what we needed to do next.

We discussed driving out to Monks' Heath, a quiet place away from the city, and then finding somewhere hidden to dump the body. After that, we would drive back to Rex's bar and start cleaning the car. The tank was just over half full of petrol, which would get us there and back.

We each cracked open another can and drank them just as quickly. Emotion was beginning to slide away from us completely.

Mo started up the car again, and we drove off. He was beginning to return to his normal self.

'My dude, skin one up. A fat one, man, and hand me the whiskey, please, bro.' he said while driving through the city roads.

We had been away from the city centre for over five minutes. The traffic was becoming less frequent. It was the early hours of the morning.

I sparked up and looked at Mo, who was still looking a little distressed. I passed him the smoke.

'Mate… Big Paddy was a terrible guy. You've done the world a fucking favour. And you saved my life. I was on the way out, man. It feels weird to say that. I could feel his hands killing me. I don't know how longer... if you hadn't pulled that trigger, then he would have killed me and probably you after. You saved me, man.' I told him.

Mo reached out his left hand, and we fist-bumped each other. Then he passed me the smoke back.

'My dude. I wasn't going to let that happen, not to you. You're my bud, man, my best. No fucking way would I have watched that. Even if I didn't have the gun, I would have gotten him off you. Fuck knows how.'

We fist-bumped again and drove further towards the outer city, calmness returning to our hearts. I was beginning to feel that everything was going to turn out okay.

Under the moon, the streetlights passed us by while a small number of vehicles made their way in and out of the city. I thought about turning my phone on and messaging Mona.

'Police!' Mo said neurotically.

'What?' I replied.

'At the back! Police! Look in your mirror!'

'What?... Shit! … Just stay calm. Drive steady, don't panic and put your fucking seat belt on, man.'

'It's the fucking feds! There's a dead geezer in the back!'

'Just calm down, Mo.'

I looked in my wing mirror. He was right. Behind us was a police car, and it was getting closer.

My heart was in my throat again. Sweat ran down the back of my neck as I started to freak out while looking at the law in the wing mirror. Hopefully, they wouldn't notice us. There was no way we would have been able to talk our way out of that one. Drunk driving with a firearm in a stolen car that had a dead body in the back. Lawfully speaking, we were fucked.

Mo sped up—not a lot, but enough to trigger a sense of suspicion as the officers turned on their blues and twos. Bright blue lights flashed in the wing mirror as the sound of their siren pierced my courage.

'Fuck this, dude, we're getting out of here.' Mo said, with a new tone of competence.

He picked up the speed.

The police closed in on our movement. Mo was overtaking cars, swerving from the left to the right of the road while dicing with a high-speed death. I firmly held onto anything I could grip hold of to try and keep balanced in the car. My eyes were shifting from the chasing police in the mirrors to the near crashes Mo was evading ahead of us.

Mo got off the main road and turned right down a side street. The police quickly tailed us. Weaving in and out, Mo drove around the suburban streets. Sweat fell down his forehead as he changed gears, swerving and drifting around corners and cars. It was incredible driving, the kind that you couldn't think too much about. He just had to act without any fear.

I tugged on my seat belt as Mo turned left and right. I didn't know if the next turn would be a dead end or a front-on collision.

The sound of the police siren still haunted our trail. We bounced off a kerb and nearly hit an oncoming car.

Mo kept driving. He nearly went head-on into a garden fence but managed to change course at the last second. The flashing blue lights were still chasing us. The thought of getting caught made me physically feel sick.

Further down the street, a small group of hooded youths dived out of the way to avoid being run down by Mo's driving. They shouted and threw beer bottles at the back of the car. A couple of them hit the boot, and the bottles smashed to pieces on impact.

The chase was bound to attract the attention of other officers. Mo swerved, and the back of the car clipped a stationary vehicle, though it didn't halt our efforts to escape. I wasn't concerned with the damage done to the car or what Rex or Ricky would say about it. I just wanted to get away from the police and away from the situation.

Mo made a turn, and we drove over a main road without hesitation, closely avoiding a collision from either side. The car's braked hard to avoid hitting us. That caused a three-car crash in our wing mirrors and created the roadblock we needed to separate us from the police. It didn't look good when I looked back.

Mo managed to get a bit of distance and then saw an opportunity. He made a right turn in front of a double-decker bus. He then took another immediate right at the end of that road and then a left to lead onto a small park.

Mo turned off the car lights and drove up the kerb onto the grass. We could see a road lit up in the distance on the other side of the park. I was hoping the park was empty. He could no longer see where he was driving with his lights off, but Mo knew that area well.

Luckily, we got over to the other side without any trouble. Then he circled around and headed back to a main road, still weaving in and out of cars as he overtook them.

'I can't see them.' I said, fixated on the wing mirror.

'Keep an eye out, man. I'm gonna get us out of here. I know where we are.' Mo replied.

'Fuck, It's weird, man. Tonight. These near-death experiences and the feds it's got me thinking. Katie, man. I think I love her. I know I've never said anything before. I can't get her out my head, ever. I've never said anything to her, man. Nothing. Too scared to ruin the friendship, dude. That would be so shit, man.' Mo admitted while still driving like a lunatic.

'Mo, that's all cool and that, but can we talk about this later, mate? Concentrate on the fucking road, yeah?' I replied hastily while holding on tight to my seat belt.

'I know, man, but really, I think I love her. Do you think she likes me?'

'Mate, now is not the fucking time!'

'What, you think I should wait a bit?'

'No, I think you should put your seatbelt on and fucking drive!'

Mo weaved in and out of cars and took several turns down the city streets to aim us back on course. We were in Fallowfield.

'Shit nearly hit a fucking kerb... I think about her all the time. We get on so well. We're always hanging, laughing, the two of us. I think it could really work. I want to be the one she can rely on, you know. To be there for her. It's not even a physical thing, man. Like, obviously, she's super-hot, but I love her mind, man. I just wanna be with her all the time; I think I should tell her about this. Tonight has made me realise I need to tell her—life's too short, man. I'm gonna tell her. What do you think?' Mo asked.

'I think you sound like a soppy prick, mate.' said a deep voice from behind me. I didn't recognise it.

I turned to look. The man from the back of the car was sat up. He threw his arms and body to the front of the car and began strangling Mo. He wasn't dead. The driving must have revived him from his alcohol coma.

I grabbed onto his wrists, trying to get him off his neck. Mo was losing control of the car. He was driving on and off the wrong side of the road, narrowly missing the oncoming traffic.

'Get the fuck off!' I screamed while hitting the guy on the side of the head with my fist. It was no good; he wasn't letting go of his neck.

Mo swerved onto the wrong side of the road and then onto the pavement. The man was still strangling him. Mo lost control of the steering wheel and drove head-on into a tree.

The man from the back of the car smashed through the windscreen while my body jolted forward as the airbags came out almost simultaneously. That made my already sore and nearly strangled-to-death neck throb with agony as my face collided with the inflated cushion.

I stayed where I was for a moment. Eyes closed. The airbags began to deflate. I could feel my face bleeding. The warm blood trickled down my cheeks.

After I had gotten over the initial blow of the crash, I slowly sat back. I hurt. Everywhere ached horrendously.

The smell of the fresh air and the smoking motor came through the broken windscreen, infiltrating my taste and smell. I looked to my right.

'Mo?' I groaned as my vision slowly began to focus. Fumes from the engine were filling the car. In my blurred vision, Mo was leant forwards on the deflating airbag.

'Mo? You alright, man?' I groaned a little louder. He still didn't have his seat belt on.

I called his name repeatedly while grabbing his shoulder. There was no reply. I pulled his head back. Blood was all down his face, his broken glasses were hanging loose, and his open eyes weren't blinking. He sat limp and silent. I tugged him back and forth, begging for a reaction.

'Mo, fucking say something! Mo, for fuck sake! Mo!' I continued to yell.

Smoke, lit by the streetlights, continued to rise from the front of the car. I pulled and shouted at him, begging him to be alive.

The smell of the smoke thickened in my blood-filled nose, and a bright light came from the crushed bonnet. The light got brighter, and the temperature rose until the flames were visible. I needed to get us both out of there.

As the fire grew, I knew I didn't have long. I screamed at Mo, pulling him harder and harder.

I reached down to my right, undid my seat belt, and then opened my door while trying to pull Mo out with me. There was no luck; I couldn't do it. His feet were caught on something.

My efforts to pull him out continued. Still, he wouldn't budge. His face was full of blood, and his glasses had fallen off.

I pulled myself out of the car and limped around to the driver's door. My body was suffering from all over. I was in the worst state of agony I had ever felt, but I didn't have time to rest. I had to get Mo out of the car.

People were driving past, but no one stopped to help. I was praying someone would pull over and get us both out of there.

I pulled and pulled at Mo's door handle, but it wouldn't open. The flames from the bonnet grew bigger. The door was jammed. I kept trying to pull it, but it wouldn't work, and I pulled so hard that my hand started to bleed. I had to fight through the pain. Still, the door wouldn't open. The handle became slippery from my blood. I couldn't get a grip of it. The only way was to try again at pulling him out of the passenger's door.

While running back around to the other side of the car, a small explosion popped out of the bonnet. I heard it late but still managed to dive onto the ground for cover. The flames got taller, and the heat was practically scorching my skin.

I turned to look at the car. The sound I heard just before the explosion signalled a second warning. I knew what was coming next.

I got to my feet and ran four strides before the car erupted with a huge explosion and flung my body through the air.

My body felt paralysed for a moment as I lay there on the path. The wind had been stolen from my lungs. The palms of my bloodstained hands were stinging with fresh cuts from the landing. All I could smell was burning petrol.

I opened my eyes and lifted my dizzy head. The car behind me was completely engulfed in flames. It was like a scene straight from hell. Every corner of the car was ablaze. The fire grew out the top, scorching the tree as it roared. There wouldn't be much time until the fire spread.
My heart broke as I realised there was no way Mo could have survived that. I sat looking at the car for a few seconds, tears falling from my face. I had to get as far away as I could.

Other cars had finally stopped. A man had come to my aid. He helped me to my feet. I got blood all over his hands. In a panic, I pushed him off and tried to run as far as I could. He shouted after me as I limped and panted down the side of the road, agony prevailing through every bone in my legs. I kept running.

After half a mile, I stopped and fell to the ground. Floods of tears came crashing down my cheeks. The salt of my tears bit into my cut face, stinging like a hundred bees.

Reality set. It filled my heart with cold concrete. Mo was gone. He had died, and it was all my fault. There was no chance of fixing it.

I sat quietly sobbing with my head in my hands for a few minutes before pulling my cigarettes out of my pocket to sit smoking at the side of the road. Cars passed as I slowly filled the street side with blood and desperation.

Then, reaching into my other pocket, I pulled out my phone. Once it was turned on, I wasn't surprised to see forty-eight missed calls and thirty-four text messages from Mona. It was time to call her. I only hoped she hadn't heard the news about her dad yet.

'Jack. What the fuck? Where have you been? I've been so worried. Are you okay? Why have you been ignoring me? Where are you?' Mona said tiredly. I must have woken her up.

'I need you to come pick me up.' I replied in a melancholy and weakened tone.

'Jack? What's wrong? Why do you sound sad? Where are you? I'll come now; tell me where you are.'

'Drive down Wilmslow Road. I'm just past Fallowfield. You'll see me.' I put the phone down. Tears of guilt trickled down my face. She tried to call me back, but I didn't answer. I just sat there, smoking and gently crying.

Once my second cigarette was finished, I got to my feet and walked towards the city centre. I'm not sure if Mona tried to call me back a third time; I had turned my phone off again. I was inconsolable.

After about twenty minutes of slow walking, I saw her car driving towards me. Her startled eyes began to cry as she pulled up next to me. I walked around to the passenger side and got in.

'What the fucks happened!?' she asked while grabbing my hands, tears falling down her cheeks.

'Just drive, please.' I replied while pulling my bloodied

hands away. Mona looked hurt by my lack of love. She turned the car around and drove towards the city centre.

'What's happened, Jack?'

I didn't know what to say.

'Jack, what's fucking happened? You look like shit. Your clothes are all dirty, and you look like you've been beaten up. Why haven't you called me? I've been sat all day, worried. What happened last night? What the fuck happened to you tonight? Where's Mo? Katie said you were with Mo?'

Tears fell down my face.

'Jack? What's wrong? Where's Mo?'

I couldn't bring myself to say it. The words wouldn't come out. I just looked ahead, thinking of Mo's happy face, telling me how much he loved Katie before the crash and all the different memories I had of Mo. The night we met. The times we played music on stage together. The laughs we had. All the weed we had smoked together while talking until the morning light. I was thinking of how different the night could have panned out if we had just done this or that differently.

'Jack! Fucking answer, stop ignoring me!'

'Mo's dead.' I whispered. It felt like a knife had sliced through my breathing as I said it.

'What? I can't hear you. Mo's what?'

'He's… he's dead! He's fucking dead. He's fucking…' I replied. Another teardrop fell down my cheek.

'What do you mean?'

'Mona, he's dead. There was a car crash and… it's... it's my fault.'

I lit a cigarette and told Mona everything. Every detail, apart from the fact that it was her dad in the yard that I had killed. I'd never heard her so quiet as she listened.

Once I had finished, floods of tears poured down her face uncontrollably as she told me that she thought Katie was madly in love with Mo too and was hoping one day soon he would make a move on her.

She turned down a side road in the city centre and parked up. Then she began to cry with her head in her hands. Mo was one of her best friends, and he was dead. Also, her boyfriend had killed someone. It was too much for her to handle.

'Jack, what if you died in that crash? I would have died too. I love you. I love you so much.' she whimpered through her tears, throwing her arms around me and kissing me repeatedly on the cheek.

We stayed cuddled like that for a minute. Then she sat back and glared at me, wide-eyed and angry. My blood was all over her.

'Dad, was with Big Paddy tonight.' she said fearfully.

I gasped. I tried to hide it, but I couldn't.

'Tell me it wasn't him.' said Mona. I didn't reply; I just looked straight ahead.

'Jack, tell me it wasn't fucking him!' she repeated. Still, I said nothing.

Mona picked her phone up from the drink holder by the gear stick and called her dad. The phone rang and rang, but there was no answer.

Then someone picked up.

'Mona. Hi, hi. How you doing? You okay? It's McDonald.' his Irish accent was strong.

'Hi, can I speak to my dad, please? Where is he?'

'Mona… Look, Mona. I don't know how t tell you tis… your dad's… Your dad's been involved in… in an accident. He's been in an accident. And I'm really sorry to tell you tis. He passed away not long ago. I'm really sorry, Mona, to be t one to tell you. Really, I am. I should have rang your mum to tell her first, but it all happened so quickly, and it's chaos here at t minute. He loved you so much, Mona and.'

Mona hung the phone up and screamed. I'd never heard anyone scream that loudly before. It was deafening. She kicked and hit whatever she could in front of her repeatedly while the screaming somehow got louder.

'It was you, wasn't it!?' she yelled while slapping me all over repeatedly.

'You fucking killed him! You killed my dad! You fucking killed him!'

'Mona, I'm sorry. I didn't mean to! He was gonna shoot Mo.' I replied while trying to shield her slaps. She was hitting all my sores.

'You fucking killed him! That was my dad! You killed him! You fucking killed him! I hate you! I fucking hate you! I fucking hate you!' She kept hitting me and screaming.

'Mona, it wasn't like that.' I felt awful, the worst I've ever felt.

'You killed him! Jackson Duke, I never want to see you again! Ever! Ever! We're done! We're fucking done! You hear me?!'

'Mona, just calm down. I didn't know it was him.'

'No, Jack! No!'

'Mona, I'm… I'm sorry.'

'I'm gonna kill you! I'm gonna fucking kill you, Jack! How could you!? Get out! Get fucking out! Get the fuck out of my car now! Now! I'm gonna kill you! I'm gonna fucking kill you, Jack! Never call me ever again! Ever! I hate you! I fucking hate you, Jack! I hate you! Get the fuck out and away from me now! Get out! Get out! Get out!' she screamed.

I opened the car door and fell out while she continued to scream and hit me. I closed the door and limped away quickly. Her crying and screaming could still be heard halfway down the street. I felt sick again. The guilt and the grief was too much to handle. My head was spinning again. I hated that I had done that to her, taken her dad from her. Both that and Mo dying broke my heart completely. I wished I could take it all back. I was desperate to start the day again but knew I couldn't. What was done was done.

I turned a corner and walked up Oxford Road. What was I to do? Mo was dead, Mona had broken up with me, Ricky was still owed a car, and I had killed someone…

As I walked through the night, the city was still in full party mode. It was nearly two in the morning. The only thing I could think to do was to go to Rex.

I banged on the door of his bar. After a moment, John opened it. The bar hadn't been closed for the night for long.

'I need to see Rex.' I told him. John let me in and then locked up again after. He told me to go to the office.

I walked upstairs, and my blood-stained knuckles knocked three times on his office door.

'Fuck off!' Rex shouted from the other side.

'It's Jack.' There was a moment of silence, and then the office door opened.

'What do you want, ya pervert? Well, come in. That was fucking quick. Take a seat. Want a drink, Lad? You look like fucking shit, mate. Really, you do. Fucking hell. Go on, sit down. Go on.'

As I sat down, Rex handed me a cold bottle of beer. I downed it in one.

'Fucking hell. What's happened then? Where's Mo?' Rex asked from the other side of his desk while handing me another beer.

I told Rex everything. Every detail about the past twenty-four hours. The money as well. He didn't say a word. He just listened.

Once I had finished, he lit another cigarette and threw the box towards me as an offering. We smoked in silence while he leant back in his chair, staring at the wall in deep thought.

Then he turned and looked me in the eyes.

'You. You're in the shit, mate. Fucked. Proper. Father time is not your friend at the minute. He is showing you how very cruel this world can be. The geezers dug you a pit, thrown you in there with all the snakes and the tigers while the Devil watches on, laughing at your struggle, mate. Caressed in your suffering. Your best friend, he's fucking dead, ain't he? Your bird, she's fucked you off because you killed her old man. Slayed the geezer where he stood. Ricky, well, you still owe that pervert a car. And, no doubt, when the O'brien's find out, and they will find out, that you're the reason their dear old godforsaken pa-pah is dead, no number of souls would rival the enjoyment that the devil will get off on when he watches them do his work on you. Truly, they are gonna fuck you up, mate. Plus, you nicked their car. And you've suddenly come into the possession of a considerable amount of cash. Whoever that belongs to is gonna wanna have a go, too.

So… The only question is. What are you to do next? Ay? Now, I'm not daft. I know you ain't a fucking clue, nor do you have a pot to piss in. Christ alive. Look at ya. But, I say to you… You need to get out of town, mate. You need to leave. Today. Take the money and fuck off down south. John aint gonna say nothing, trust me on that. Neither will the lads that picked you up earlier. Not if they don't want John to cut out their fucking tongues. But you, you need to leave this city and start again. Alright? Tell no one where you've been, where you've come from or where you're fucking going. Apart from me. Join the army, maybe. Actually, yeah… brilliant idea. Join the fucking Para Reg. They'll sort you out, see that you're right. Mega. Use that cash to rent you a room somewhere and sign up to join the Queen's finest. Memorise my phone number, Jack, and my number only. Then, throw your phone deep into the river. That's the best chance you've got, mate.'

'The army?' I replied, startled at the idea, before swigging my beer.

'Yes. The army. And, not just any Regiment, The Parachute Regiment. They're the fucking best, Jack. They're an elite fucking unit of ferocious professionals.

And, seen as you've already killed one geezer, you'll find the next one easy, won't ya?… You'll have to work hard every day. They'll push you in ways you didn't know you could be pushed. But you can do it.'

I didn't reply.

'Honestly, Jack, I think that's your best bet. You need somewhere to lie low for a while and they will offer you a chance at greatness. What else you gonna do? Do some dead-end job in some shit-house town, always looking over your shoulder that some geezers come to finish you off? Or you could be a soldier, and an elite fucking soldier at that, protected behind the fences of a military camp with a band of brothers, learning how to fuck geezers up with guns and grenades. It could be the making of ya, ya mad little pervert. What do you reckon?'

'Sounds… yeah, you're probably right.'

'Course I fucking am. Course… Now, go on then, fuck off. You need to get out of town quick time. And keep in touch. I wanna hear from you on a regular, alright? I'll come down and see you when I get chance. If you need anything, then I am here, Jack. Just gimme a call, and I'll sort it. Anything.'

I looked Rex in the eyes, trying to compose myself. It was all so overwhelming.

'Rex. Thank you for everything. You've been a bit like a…' Rex put his hand out to stop me from continuing.

'Don't say another word, Jack. Let's not get fucking weird in here. I know what you were gonna say, and I understand. You're a good lad, Jack, truly. Now, go out that door and leave this city in the past. May the horrors of the last twenty-four hours never catch up with you. Bloody hell, all the difference a day can make ay? Jesus. Let me know how you get on. I'll look forward to hearing from ya. Now go on, fuck off before they get to ya.'

I looked Rex in the eye and nodded again. Then he looked at the door and then back at me to signal that it was time to leave.

When I got to the door, he said

'Jack, you can have these. But stay off the weed if you're going in the army.' He threw a pack of cigarettes at me.

Within minutes, I was back in the street, heading to my flat. It didn't take long to get home. My head was swimming in a million different thoughts.

I showered again and packed some essentials and a few changes of clothes into the gym bag that had the money in it. Then, I headed to the train station and waited there to catch the first train down south.

Rex was right. And his idea seemed to be my best option. It would keep me out of trouble. I didn't know the first thing about the army or the Parachute Regiment.

I couldn't get Mo and Mona out of my head. They were the biggest parts of my life, and I was never going to see them again. Tears fell down my face. I wiped them away and picked up my bag to board the train.

I got the first train to Leicester and then rented a room in a house. The army recruitment centre said joining would take up to three months. That gave me enough time to get fit.

I woke up every day and ran—miles and miles I covered. Then, in the afternoon, I went to the gym. I barely had a day's rest. Other than that, I would go back to my rented room and read as many books as I could to try and escape my thoughts.

Mo Was gone, but he was never forgotten. It took a long time for it to sink in. I didn't smile or laugh for months. Nightmares of that night tormented my sleep and woke me in a pool of cold sweat. Everything everywhere reminded me of either him or Mona, and then they would remind me of the other. Every record I heard. Every bar I walked by. Every car I saw. Every handholding couple. I missed her. I missed them both. I recluse from the world, and I hid from the noise, from the music. The lonesome guilt of depression had swallowed me whole. I was the sky in rose at dawn to rust and ruin.

After three months of gruelling training, I was on the train to Darlington with a shaved head. That was where I met the rest of my platoon and boarded the coach to Catterick, where I would start my new life with the Parachute Regiment Training Company."

Chapter Seven

It took a lot for Jack to talk about what happened. He looked at the rain pouring down on the window and concentrated on his breathing but tried not to make his discomfort obvious. It was hard for him to relive those emotions. However, he knew what came next was equally, if not harder, to say aloud. He was also confused about how the man opposite him seemed to know so much, though Jack's patience prevailed.

"Back to the night that Mindy was killed.

Four meters of water stretched between the riverbanks. On one side were the meadows, and on the other was a second field where the dusty and weathered house from the Polaroid photograph stood.

As I crossed, with my rifle raised above my head, only from my chest up managed to stay dry. The water was cold, and that old, murky, dirty river smell latched onto me. I knew it would be with me for the duration of the morning. That was the least of my worries. I was used to operating in a state of sopping misery; you spend most of your army career wet and freezing. I'd like to say you get used to it, but you don't. Nevertheless, they were familiar conditions in which I was trained to work in and were no hindrance. I had tunnel vision on getting Isla back.

The old house from the Polaroid photograph was in view. It was over five hundred meters away, on the other side of the overgrown grassy field I had just crossed over to. Three cars were parked on the property to the right of the house. A ray of light shone from a lone bottom-floor window, softly illuminating the field in front of it—a mirror to the darkness of the night outside.

I was trying to stay calm, but not knowing the depths of Isla's danger made it hard to decompartmentalise. I needed to get a grip, or I would have been no use to her at all, but my head was struggling. Uncertainty grew like a tumour, spreading and poisoning my thoughts. Make no mistake, I was confident in my abilities. There was no doubt that I would get her back and bring justice to those who were involved, whoever they were. But I was fucking terrified of losing her.

Walking slowly along the riverbank, I took cover in the shadows of the trees that grew along the water, being careful not to compromise my position.

In the distance, the door of the house opened. An automatic porch light brightened the night ahead, giving a fuller view of the surrounding area, which was bigger than I first thought. The front door looked directly onto the field. If it wasn't for the cover of the trees, I would have been spotted with ease. I slowly lowered myself into the prone position next to a tree trunk and used my rifle's LDS scope to try and get a better look at who was standing in the doorway.

It was a woman, though she wasn't looking in my direction. She was looking out onto the open field and around the edges of the driveway. Bushes surrounded the front garden; they were just low enough to see her from her torso up. Something about her silhouette seemed hauntingly familiar.

The woman turned and went back inside, shutting the door behind her. The porch light stayed lit. I began to leopard crawl along the field towards the house, checking the situation ahead through the rifle's scope every five meters.

The long, thin, lone road that led to the house, lined with waist-high bushes that acted as a garden fence for the property, separated the field that I was in from the house. The road was connected to a bridge that crossed the weir. The weir then led onto the meadows, though bollards stopped cars from being able to pass that far.

The house was built directly next to the widest part of the river. It had a huge garden surrounding the back and the right of it, with trees and bushes securing the privacy of the perimeter. There was no access to the left side of the house from the meadows—not without swimming. Also, there was no gate at the front, just an opening into the carpark on the right side of the house, big enough to comfortably fit a car through.

The porch light had turned itself off. I continued to crawl until I reached the road, thankful the overgrown grass was free of rocks.

Once I'd checked that the area was clear of personnel, I quickly dashed across the road and got back down behind a bush in the front garden to observe the house in closer detail. There was nothing to hear or see, and there was no activity coming from within the parked cars, either.

After analysing the imminent threat level, I decided to make a move along the bushes to the side of the building, trying to avoid the front door's light sensor.

I reached the left wall of the house, the side that ran along the river. Staying tight to the brickwork, I manoeuvred along the riverbank towards the back garden, again using the darkness for cover.

Creeping with care through the abyss, my rifle led the way, aimed and ready. The safety catch was off, and my finger teased at the trigger. All my senses were heightened to react at the scratch of a second with maximum violence.

On the riverbank, I got down low to turn the corner of the house, checking before tactically advancing into the back garden. There was nothing obvious to be seen, but there was no way of knowing what lurked in the distance. The back garden was black from the shadows of trees. Not even the moonlight lived there.

Sneaking brick tight around the back of the house, I reached a white windowless door and alluded to the thought of a possible trap. The use of it wasn't an option. It felt too obvious. Maybe that was the game they wanted me to play. I needed to have a better understanding of the area before I made a move, and then I could plan the attack.

Onwards, I went, with a crouched stance, as I moved slowly across the back wall of the house. I came to a window that was higher up than normal but still on the bottom floor. There was no light coming from it. I crouched even lower to pass underneath it.

Then, a loud smash came from the front of the house as if someone had dropped and shattered a drinking glass. Something snapped on the ground behind me. I quickly turned, but it was too late…"

-

"When I woke up, I was slumped back in a chair in front of a square wooden table in an old, run-down kitchen. The walls and furnishings were dirty and dated, and there were cobwebs in the corners of the ceiling.

I had been hit hard around the head, and the force of it had knocked me unconscious. The side of my skull ached, and my eyes were a slight blur.

My hands were untied, but my rifle was gone, and my jacket had been removed. I couldn't feel the spare ammunition in the back pockets of my river-soaked jeans either, nor could I see the shape of my phone and keys.

As my eyes regained focus and adjusted to the dim, superficial light, I began to recognise the three people ahead.

Sat opposite me, casually smoking a cigarette, was an aged and grey Conor O'Brien. His unblinking eyes were fixed on me. We'd never formally met before, but pretty much everyone in Manchester knew what the O'Briens looked like. I had seen him and his wife out when I lived in the city. I was walking with Mona, and the cousins happily greeted each other, though their interaction was nothing more than a wave and a smile.

You could tell Conor was a man with money from how he dressed, though there was nothing particularly smart about his designer appearance. He wore a dark-coloured, quality-looking jacket on top of a thick, plain black T-shirt, and an expensive-looking golden watch was fastened around his left wrist.

Stood to the right of him, looking just as beautiful as the last time I saw her and stunningly youthful for a woman in her mid-thirties, was a wide-eyed and arms-folded Mona O'Brien. It was annoying how good she looked in her thin, tightly fitted white T-shirt that angelically complimented her olive skin. It seemed like she hadn't gained even a kilogram in fourteen years. Her denim blue jean waist was tiny. She was staring at me. They all were.

Mona's intense gaze suggested a dozen different cries of emotion. She was calm, but her quick breathing was noticeable. She was finding the rage flickering within hard to hide; that much was obvious.

It felt both incredible and devastating to see her again. I never would have thought I would hate her, ever. But there she was; she'd taken Isla and was involved with the slaughtering of my wife. I hated her. I hated them all. I had to keep my cool and be free from emotion.

Stood to the left of Conor, lazily pointing the barrel of his AK47 rifle in the direction of my chest, was someone who I thought and hoped never to see again. An old army comrade of mine. Jonathan Allen."

Chapter Eight

"2007.

The coach to Catterick Garrison was an unsettling journey. The shaven heads of tough-looking and frightened young men silently filled the seats while two angry Parachute Regiment corporals inflicted fear from the front.

I didn't know what to expect. I knew nothing about the army before enlisting. I had done a little research on the computer at the library in Leicester and had read a few books, though nothing could have prepared me for Para Depot.

Barbed wire fences and army trucks, marching men and distantly relentless gunfire cemented the reality of entrapment as the coach went through the gates of the camp.

We drove past the parade square on the way to the barracks, where many hardened men had had their passing out ceremony to ascend their honour to monumental heights after proving their worth to join the elite fighting force—the Parachute Regiment.

The shock of capture had set in instantly. Fifty-eight of us stood straight and tall in rows of three in front of the barracks with all our bags and ironing boards at our feet. That was to be our home for the next six months.

Cold rain poured down on our civilian suits while the Sergeant impressed upon us the intimidating reality that only eight men who stood before him would make it to the end and become lifelong members of their regiment. Many would quit, many would transfer to less elite regiments, and most would become injured sooner or later. That was the nature of the beast that we were to be bitten by.

As we stood there, enduring the rain like we'd never suffered before, unable to shelter from the falling heavens,

I knew I wasn't the only one thinking I'd made a mistake. Our lives were no longer our own. We had become just a number and belonged to both Queen and country, ready to learn how to take and defend life for the greater good of a nation. I felt sick, but I tried to show a brave face and not be shackled by the fear.

We were stripped of our names and identities and then were given a new name, Joe, which stood for 'Joined On Enlistment'. Collectively and individually, that is what we were to be called for the duration of our time at Para Depot. On the rare occasions that we were to be addressed on a more personal level, only our surnames existed. I was thankful for that, as 'Jack' was a military term for someone who either quits or does a shit job at something. Daily we would hear the training team shouting at us that we 'shouldn't Jack on our mates', or 'don't be, Jack', and 'you Jack shit'. To be or to do 'Jack' was a terrible sin.

To my comrades and superiors, I was known as Duke, Private Duke. Becoming a private gave me immense pride. It was as if, almost immediately, I had found a purpose in life away from the madness of Manchester, though I missed my old life.

Six days later, after nearly a week of paperwork, medicals and briefs, we had our first physical test out on the back hills of North Yorkshire.

'Just a four-mile run.' the Physical Training Instructor told us. That was not how it panned out. Six fit and strong young lads out of fifty-eight collapsed, and one became momentarily unconscious due to being pushed to a level of exhaustion that our bodies hadn't suffered before. I had never experienced anything as tough as that first run, and by that point, I had built up a near-athlete level of fitness. The smallest hill we had to sprint up was around six storeys high, with roughly a fifty-degree incline. We had to run up and down, time after time again, while the training team swore aggressively at us to work harder and to move quicker.

One of the PTIs grabbed a young Joe by the throat and screamed in his face for smiling at another recruit. Because of that, we were all made to do push-ups in the rocky dirt. One of the Joe's wasn't lowering his body enough at the bottom, so the same PTI stamped his foot down on the young Joe's ankle and made us all do even more push-ups.

From then on, each day only got tougher as we were pushed harder and harder to surpass levels of resilience that we didn't know were humanly possible. Crawling through flooded trenches bedded with sharp rocks and physical events such as the log and stretcher races, the corridor sessions, the steeple chase, and the two-miler were all horrendously gruelling and devastatingly painful to participate in, but all simulated the efforts that were needed to be replicated out on the battlefield.

They were preparing us for serious business. War. And war is, as I later found out, no fucking game. It's not easy, and mistakes or weaknesses will indefinitely lead to permanent catastrophes. People will die; that is war.

We were practising and training at such intensity to ensure competence and triumph over the enemy. The real thing awaited us at the end of our time at Depot. We were being trained for the fight in the Middle East.

The volume of work we regularly achieved in eighteen-hour days and the magnitude of energy and concertation we had to deliver off three to five hours of sleep each night hit a lot of the recruits hard, especially me. Before the eighth week, ten men had quit, and another eight were on crutches.

It's cold and miserable most of the year in the UK, and the terrain you have to sleep in and crawl through is always sopping wet with rocky mud. If you can administer yourself, survive and fight in those conditions, you can do it anywhere. The enemy doesn't give a fuck that you're wet, cold and tired. They will come for you.

Para Depot was tough, not just for me but for everyone. It was a world away from my drug-induced life in Manchester. You have to wake up and get on with it.

You can hear the rain crashing down on the roof of your basher and the cold wind blowing through the open sides. It's tough to crawl out of a warm sleeping bag and get changed back into your soaking-wet fighting clothes in the dark of a freezing night without the aid of a torch to see where your equipment is.

It's hard learning to do every stationary task on a knee without knee pads. It's hard to tab miles with over forty pounds of kit on your back. It's hard to conduct your drills at battle-fighting speed and to carry on when morale is low. It's hard to operate competently while being sleep-deprived for weeks with hands that are frozen cold and full of cuts and tears.

I often thought of quitting. I often wanted to hand in my letter to discharge from the military. But I kept going. The thought that Mona had told her cousins all the details and that I was a wanted man by the biggest crime family in Manchester was enough motivation to push me through the pain. As weird as it sounded, I was safe in the army. They couldn't get to me there. The army would have been the last place anyone would have looked for me.

Every day was a new kind of excruciating level of pain. But at the end of it all, none of it would have meant a thing if I hadn't passed the regimental test, P company.

By that point, your fitness levels are capable. But make no mistake; there is a reason why, on average, only ten per cent of those who start on day one get to wear the maroon beret. Without passing P company, you are unable to join the Parachute Regiment and must transfer to another regiment. Just like many of my mates had to. Just like Johnny Allen had to.

From the moment I met Jonathan Geoffrey Allen, I knew we wouldn't be friends. He was a total twat. Allen was a couple of years older, a couple of inches taller and quite a bit bigger than me. He came from an upper-class background where a silver spoon had fed his appetite for a false sense of self-righteousness.

He would mouth off when we were lined up in the corridor or the dinner cue for the scoff house, showing a total disregard for respect and discipline. That always resulted in the rest of the platoon suffering the punishment of a 'beasting'.

Allen would constantly Jack on others to get ahead, while trying whenever he could to make himself look better in front of the training team. They saw straight through him.

A few times, he wiped his arse on the other lad's pillows, and he would bang cupboard doors to close them while the lads were trying to get some sleep before reveille at half five in the morning.

When it was time to do the morning cleaning jobs around the block, Allen was always nowhere to be seen. He wasn't a team player. Things were hard enough for everyone, and he would forever be trying to make it harder.

There was a suspicion of him stealing cigarettes, lighters and other things from our platoon and hiding stuff, too, like belts and water bottles. Maybe he did it so that others would either fall behind or receive punishment from the corporals. You'd get a bollocking if you lost a piece of issued kit, a proper bollocking.

He was a sadistic twat. We'd compete against each other at every effort we could, and often, I would come out as the victor; he hated that.

He refused to wake up for his stag duty on an early exercise, two nights a row, Jacking completely on me and the rest of the platoon. The Joe who went to wake him up the first time didn't wait with him while he got changed back into his wet fighting gear. Instead, the Joe left Allen's side and went to find his own basher area to get some sleep. When that happened, I was left on the sentry position, alone and unable to be relieved, as the sentry position needed to be manned at all times in case of enemy invasion. I got fuck all sleep that night.

Allen would bully the smaller and younger recruits. I hit him for it once. I was defending a lad. Allen tore the top of the young lad's family photograph, so I twatted him in the nose. Blood sprayed out everywhere. His nose was never the same after that.

He was the anchor, dragging the morale down. He never screwed the nut. I hated him. There's no way I would have wanted a man like him next to me on the battlefield. He would have gotten us all killed. We couldn't have relied on him.

He failed P company, twice so I heard. That meant he had to transfer to a different regiment like the lizard he was. I don't know where he went. I forgot all about him.

I did, unfortunately, see Johnny Allen again. It was when I was twenty-eight, at the Army vs Navy rugby match. I spoke to him briefly. He was with his wife, a pretty blonde woman. Allen was off his face, drunk and high on cocaine. His wife was visibly annoyed with him. He was an embarrassment—a fucking state. She had every right to be pissed off.

He told me that he blamed me for not passing P company and not fulfilling his life's dream of joining the Parachute Regiment. I told him that was fucking absurd, and that I refused to take responsibility for his incompetence, and that the only matter that I would honourably take responsibility for was the state of his fucking nose.

That resulted in the giant man trying to swing a punch at me. I dodged it and caught him on the nose again. His wife then turned and walked away as he watched from the ground in a hopeless state of blood and despair. That was the beginning of his divorce.

His wife was called Sophie. I bumped into her later that night at a bar. She told me a few of his dirty secrets. Apparently, Allen had spoken about me before, a few times. He was borderline obsessed with delusions. He was using steroids and had a cocaine problem, too. If the army found out about either, they would have kicked him out of the military.

I sat with her while she started to cry. She told me she was desperate for a child, just not with Allen. She'd fallen out of love with him but had never seen anyone stand up to him before I knocked him to the ground earlier that day.

Sophie stopped crying and grabbed my hand with both of hers. The drunken women slowly leant in for a kiss. I pressed my index finger to her lips and shook my head. Sophie was very beautiful, but I knew where that kiss led. I knew that wouldn't have been the right thing to do.

I comforted her tears for a little longer while being a pair of ears to listen to her grief. She had a lot that she needed to get off her chest. Then I walked her to a taxi and wished her well before giving the driver some cash to pay for her journey.

Six months later, I was told that Allen failed a compulsory and random military drug test, which led to him being dismissed from the army. The failed test and the divorce with his wife had become too much for him to handle. They said he drank himself into oblivion and just took off. No one had seen or heard from him since."

Chapter Nine

"When I woke to see the three of them, Mona, Conor O'Brien and Allen, I pretended to be unfazed by Allen's pointing rifle as I sat outnumbered at the kitchen table and tried to look more weakened and hurt than I really was, lowering them into a false sense of security and enhancing the element of surprise for when the opportune moment came to attack.

I gently rubbed my injured head to disguise my analysis of the room, turning my neck to make it appear like I was stretching away the pain.

It was a large, basic kitchen—dirty and old. A few meters to my right was an open, slightly cracked blue door leading to the hallway. Opposite the kitchen door was the front door, which was off-white, windowless, and without a letter plate.

Next to the blue kitchen door was the cooker and sink. Neither appeared to have been used in years. They were both stained and filthy, and one of the cupboard doors beneath the sink was half hanging off. The hobs on the cooker were rusted, and two of the dials that managed the heat were missing.

Above was a large dusty window. That must have been the one that looked onto the field. It had a dirty set of raised blinds to show the darkness of night; it was full of cobwebs and had a cord hanging from the right-hand side that would have once been white.

Behind me was a worktop and a set of cupboards and drawers, with a filthy old microwave and a stainless-steel kettle on top. The surface was scattered with newspapers, magazines and letters. A thick layer of dust completely hid the worktop's colour and some of the magazine details.

In the left corner behind me, standing tall and dead from power, was a fridge freezer with magnets from places visited on it.

A second door was on the left wall. It was in the same style and condition as the front door. That must have been the back door that led onto the back garden. Maybe that was the way they brought me in.

The wall in front of me was bare, apart from a large landscape painting that hung slanted in the centre, just above Connor O'Brien's head. The painting was beautiful. If clean, I imagined the colours would have perfectly complimented the painted scene. It reminded me of when Mona and I used to paint while we were stoned.

Conor was blowing cigarette smoke in my face as I studied the painting.

'Jackson Duke. I've been looking forward to this moment for quite some time. Many years, in fact.' he said while putting his cigarette out on the dusty tabletop in front of him. It looked like he had smoked half a pack since being there. The ends were scattered around the centre in front of him.

'Am I meant to know who you are, mate? Mona, you look well. Allen… fucking lizard.' I grunted, pretending to be in pain. I knew perfectly well who Conor was, but I didn't want to give him that satisfaction.

'My name is Conor, Conor O'Brien. You caused me and my family a lot of grief a few years back. Well over a decade ago now, actually. But I am not a man who lets time get in the way of justice. And my brothers and I swore that we would bring our own personal adaptation of justice to your domain. You could imagine our enjoyment in learning that we weren't the only ones who wanted to watch your world burn, Jack. We know you have money and a lot of it, though we don't quite understand how it is that you've become such a wealthy man. Nevertheless, we want it, all of it. Out of interest, Jack, not that it matters, but what is it you do for work these days?' Conor said calmly before lighting another cigarette.

Allen's rifle hadn't moved an inch the whole time. I gently gestured with my hands to ask for a cigarette, to which Conor pulled one out of the packet and threw it on the table in front of me. He then slid a golden Zippo lighter engraved *O'Brien* across the table.

'Are you married, Mr Obrien? Children?' I asked while blowing the dust off the cigarette. I had a taunting smirk on my face after making it obvious that I had seen his golden wedding ring. Conor didn't reply; he just glared at me with a stern serenity.

I put the cigarette in my mouth and went to light it, but instead, I stopped and asked Johnny Allen the same question.

'What about you, Johnny? Married? Kids?' His eyes widened at my provocation, though he remained silent. His rifle was still aimed at my chest.

Allen looked like he had put on a bit of weight over the past few years. The big man had got even bigger. Fatter. He had a slight stubble and long hair. The blonde locks fell from a middle parting and were tucked behind his ears. His eyes looked tired, and his face hadn't aged well. He looked like a man who should have been successful but wasn't.

'What about you, Mona? Married?' I asked her while teasing the cigarette around my lips again as if I was about to light it. A single tear began to form in the corner of her left eye and then fell down her cheek. A scowl grew on her perfect face as that familiar psychotic expression, the one that I knew so well, hauntingly looked through me with daggers for eyes. The nostalgia of seeing her aged eyes unsettled me. She still looked just as beautiful. Her hair hadn't changed at all, either. I imagined she dyed it. I would have guessed she was barely thirty if I didn't know her age.

'How's your wife, Jack?' she replied as if it pained her to speak the word wife. That hurt. The skin on my arms and down my back felt like it was crawling as I thought of a world without my Mindy in it.

'She was exceptional.' I replied quietly while looking Mona directly in the eyes. She appeared to be visibly distressed by my response.

So much had happened over the previous fourteen years, yet looking at her, it felt so surreal to see her, as if it was only yesterday that I had seen her last.

Then I remembered Mo. The guilt of his death weighed over me like it had done for so many years. I could hear his laughter. I hadn't thought about him properly for a while, not since that anniversary of the night he died the year before. I often wondered throughout the years how Mo would have ended up and where he would have gotten to. Maybe he would have been playing bass in a big-time band and touring the world. Whatever he would have done, I know he would have been happy. That was Mo. He was a joyous symbol of hope.

I figured they wanted me alive, at least for a little while longer. It was a game that they were playing, or they would have killed me already. They needed me alive to witness my suffering and to learn where my money was kept.

I turned my attention back to Allen. To taunt him, to learn from him, and to distract me from nostalgia.

'What happened to you then, Allen? Last I saw of you, well, I put you on your arse. Peculiar birthmark your wife, or ex-wife, has on her lower back. Looks a bit like a bird. That's the closest you've ever been to a pair of fucking wings, ain't it, mate?'

'How do you know about that?' Allen replied angrily. He had broken already. He tightened his grip in a rage and pointed the rifle at my head. That made me lower my cigarette, again preventing me from lighting it just as I wanted. I wanted them to get used to my hands being busy so that when the opportune moment arrived, I could strike without giving them too much of a warning.

'Easy.' Conor told Allen in an ordering effort to calm him down. I already knew, but it was clear who was in charge.

'Where's Isla?' I asked Conor in an assertive tone. He showed no emotion on his smoking face. Before he had time to answer there was a creak from the corridor beyond the kitchen door.

'Isla? Isla misses her daddy.' Conor replied coldly.

'Is that her out there?' I asked calmly, ready to pounce around the end of Allen's barrel to disarm him.

Conor took a big drag of his cigarette. He never broke eye contact with me.

'It took a long time for us to find you, Jack. A lot longer than I had hoped. Your vanishment was rather extraordinary. We did get a bit of help, though. A little tip-off a few months back. Some say you should be careful what you tell your friends today because tomorrow, well, tomorrow, they could be the enemy. The ones you think you can trust the most, they're usually the ones who are capable of the most devastating harm. The thing about secrets is, well, that the dirtier the secret, the more it needs to be kept. Wouldn't you agree, Jack?' said Conor.

'I don't have a fucking clue what you're going on about, mate. Whose house is this anyway?' I replied.

'I thought as much...' Conor didn't have the chance to finish what he was going to say; Mona butted in emotionally.

'My dad, Jack! My fucking dad! You fucking killed him! You killed them both, him and Paddy, and then you fucked off and left me all alone! How could you!?... Why the fuck would?... You just took off! You could have had my car! I would have given it to you; you know I would! You left me all alone when I needed you most and fucked off to apparently join the fucking army! Why would you have gone there!? I didn't know anything! Nothing about you until a few months ago! I didn't know if you'd died! Nothing! The fucking army, Jack, really!? What the fuck!? You were my everything! I loved you so much, and then you left me all alone to deal with it all after fucking killing him! Then I find out you marry some fucking redhead bitch! Why didn't you come back for me, Jack!? Why did you never come back!?' She was trying hard to fight back the tears. She uncrossed her arms briefly while talking, and I saw on the inside of her right forearm the tattoo of the Bruce Springsteen lyric.

'Mona, it wasn't like that. I didn't know it was him. I couldn't see who it was. And he was gonna shoot Mo. Then probably me straight after. I couldn't let that happen. I just swung at a shadow. Also, you told me to leave. You told me you never wanted to see me again. You made that pretty clear. I couldn't stay in the city. You know I couldn't.'

Tears fell from Mona's eyes.

'Fuck you, Jack! That's absolute bullshit! My dad was a good man! And you and me, we were meant to… we were supposed to… you wasn't meant to actually fucking leave! How could you!? You were supposed to marry me, not her! You was supposed to look after me, not her! Fourteen fucking years, Jack! Every year, I thought you'd come, but you never did! Why didn't you come back!?' Mona screamed before trying to dive over the table to attack me with her hands. Conor anticipated her rage and managed to hold her back.

'Not now, Mona.' Conor told his cousin, trying to calm her down. Mona turned and faced the wall. Her head was in her hands as she cried quietly into them. I could see the shape of a pistol behind her t-shirt; it was tucked into the back of her waist.

I felt guilty. She was right. I had promised her so many things—marriage, kids, growing old together. We were inseparable. But what I felt most guilty about was that I had lived one hundred lives since then. I'd moved on. And it had all apparently been eating up at her for fourteen years. It had stopped her from living. I also felt guilty that my love for Mindy was more in every way than it ever was for Mona.

I teased the idea of lighting the cigarette again by pressing it to my lips, but then I stopped to ask.

'How do you three know each other anyway? I get you two are cousins. Allen, where do you come into all of this?'

'You fucked up everything for me, Duke. I was to be a Para, and you took that from me. My wife left me because of you. When Mona contacted me to help her and her cousins come up with a plan, I said I would only help if I was the one who got to kill you. I know you've got money, and I want it.' Johnny Allen said, still pointing his rifle at my chest.

'Jesus. You really think that too, don't you? Fucking hell. Screw the fucking nut, you absolute hat. You still high or something? You failing P company had nothing to do with me, mate, or the fact that you're an arsehole. You kidnap a child and murder two women for that?'

'I didn't do the shooting, though I happily watched. You told the corporals a load bollocks about me. Fed them lies. I passed every event in P company, but because of you, they fucked me off!'

'What? I didn't say fuck all. I didn't need to. You made yourself look a dickhead on your own, mate. You're good at that. You didn't need my help, lizard. And you didn't pass all the events on P company; I was fucking there. I saw. You fucked it up. You were never Para Reg. Didn't have it in ya. The lads would have eaten you alive. They would have seen straight through you like the crap hat you fucking are, mate.'

'That's bollocks. You fucked me over!' Allen replied angrily.

'I didn't give you any cocaine, mate.'

'How do you know about that?'

'Your ex-wife, Sophie, she told me. Said you used to make her call you corporal during sex, too. And that you would tell people on holiday that you were Para Reg. Jesus, mate. The audacity of it, pretending to be one of us. Fucking loser.'

'Shut the fuck up!' shouted Allen, angrily pointing the barrel at my head.

'Easy Johnny.' said Conor, ordering Allen to calm down again.

I put the cigarette to my mouth and lit it that time, then slid the lighter back in front of Conor.

'Shall we stop this fucking about then? What exactly is it that you want?' I asked.

'We've already told you that. To watch your world burn. Just like you did ours.' Mona replied.

'I didn't watch, nor did I fucking burn anything, Mona. I'm sorry about your dad. Really, I am. And Paddy, well, Mo shot him while the big fucker tried to strangle me to death. And you, Allen. Fuck sake. The only thing you can blame me for is that fucking nose of yours.'

A noise creaked from the corridor again.

'Who's out there? Where's Isla? Is that her? Show me that she's okay!' I demanded.

'Isla's not here, Jack. I do hope she is okay, though.' said Conor sarcastically.

'I swear if you've hurt her, I won't just fucking kill ya. The suffering you will all endure will be fucking animal, mate.'

'Jack. We hold all the cards, my friend. And you will do exactly as we say if you ever want to see your little girl again. I doubt you'll ever see her smile the same, though.' Conor said with a sinister smirk.

'You never did tell me how the fuck you three know each other. This help you were on about. Who is it?'

'That's the funny thing, Jack. It's been right under your nose the whole time.' said Conor, smoke rising from his smile.

'Don't mention noses in front of him, mate; he'll get emotional. The state of it.' I said while gesturing my cigarette in the direction of Johnny Allen's broken face.

'You wait and see what I'm gonna do to your little girl's face, mate. I might even make you watch.' said Allen.

I was triggered. Massively. I was so close to losing my cool completely and going straight for Allen's neck. But I had to stay calm. I couldn't let emotion interfere, or I'd be certain to fail. I smoked my cigarette and concentrated on my breathing.

'Cut the shit, just get on with it and tell me.' I said.

'I think you're going to like this.' said Conor.

Mona wiped away her tears and took a few steps into the corridor. She nodded at someone down the hall. Footsteps sounded as Mona returned to the room. Following her was someone I would never have imagined to see. I couldn't hide the shock. I couldn't control my anger. The lies I had been fed. The way I had been played and deceived. I couldn't understand. Stood in the doorway and covered in blood was Cara.

I glared at the mother of my child as she stood there quietly, crying at me. I thought she was dead. She was next to Mindy in the back garden.

A desperate thought was teased around my head. Was Mindy in on it, too? She can't have been. I checked her body. There was a gunshot wound. I checked her pulse. Mindy was dead. I was sure of it. I never checked if Cara was dead, though. I was too distracted by the Polaroid photograph with Isla's name on it.

'What the fuck is going on?' I asked the room.

'Cara!? What have you done? Where's Isla?' I asked again.

Cara looked into my eyes. Tears were pouring down her face. She looked horrific. Ill. Her long dark hair was messily tied back in a ponytail. It must have been Mindy's blood that was all over her grey hoodie, leggings and trainers. I felt sick.

I raised my eyebrows to demand an answer from her.

'I couldn't bear it anymore, Jack.' Cara said quietly, struggling to speak through her tears. I thought she might have had a little bit to drink, too. She was in a world of emotional pain, that much was easy to see. Though I had never seen her so distressed before. She looked like a prisoner of war who had just been freed after months of torture.

'Couldn't bear what? What are you talking about?' I asked.

'I thought I could hide it. I thought I'd get over it, but I couldn't. I couldn't take it anymore. For years, it's just kept… just kept eating up at me. It's all too much. It's been you, and only you, since the night we met. I couldn't bear the way you looked at her. The way you looked at each other. The way you held each other all the fucking time. I thought originally that me falling pregnant would have changed things, that you would have felt differently about Mindy and would have felt something more for me. But instead, you proposed to her. I was so fucking hurt. I tried to pretend I didn't care, but it… it physically hurt me watching you two say your vows that day. And each day after that, nothing has changed. Every time I saw you two together. Every breakfast, every dinner, every fucking night when you two would be cuddled up on the sofa, laughing and kissing, and I'd be sat on the other sofa all alone, drinking my way through a bottle. And the way Isla adored Mindy, too. I felt like I could be replaced, just like that, and she would take my little girl, and you three would live happily ever after. It drove me crazy. Like fucking mental, Jack. I used to fantasise about killing you both and running away with Isla and taking all the money if I knew where it was—starting again fresh somewhere. That's what this is. I just wanted you to look at me the way you looked at her, just once. When I finally accepted that it wasn't going to happen, I knew I had to do something. When you were drunk a few years ago, I remembered you telling me about Johnny Allen and Mona and the O'Brien's. Mona was easy to find online. I barely had to do anything. She sorted everything. She's been so lovely over the past few months. A great friend.' said Cara, tears rapidly falling down her cheeks. She put her hands to her crying face. She was definitely drunk. She was struggling to stand straight.

'Cara… why's this the first I've heard about any of this? Mindy and I loved you. You were like a sister to her, to us both. How could you? To her? You've known her since you were both three years old. We gave you a house to live in. Food. Money. Fucking everything. We gave you everything, Cara… You betrayed her. You betrayed both of us. Where the fuck is Isla? Is she safe!? Where the fuck is she!?'

'Of course, she's safe.' Cara replied angrily.

Then Mona reached to the back of her jeans and pulled out the pistol with a silencer attached. In an instant, she pointed it to Cara's head and pulled the trigger. Fragments of the inside of Cara's head blew out the other side of her skull. Blood sprayed out across the dirty magnolia walls to her side and all over the oven hobs.

I had seen many people being fatally shot before, but that one hit me hard. That one rocked me like none had before. I had lived with the women for years. She was my family. I shared a daughter with her.

Cara's body slowly dropped to the ground in a heap on the floor. As she fell, her eyes never left mine. There was fear, sadness and a realisation in her dying stare. She almost looked apologetic.

I sat there, looking at the body on the floor while Mona stood over her.

'Of course, your little girl isn't safe.' Mona said softly before firing two more shots into the back of Cara's head.

Mona then turned and looked at me with a twisted smile. That same psychotic smile from my past. She began to laugh hysterically.

Conor O'Brien sparked up another cigarette, and the three of them put their full attention on me. I slowly turned away from Cara's dead body to face them. I was Angry. I felt like a fool for being played by someone I thought I could trust, who I had given everything to.

'He who fights by the sword, mate.' Conor said arrogantly. He looked victorious in my defeat and was laughing quietly to himself. He was right. He had won. His own personal adaptation of justice was being delivered to my imminent demise. I had no way out. Well, nearly no way.

Then, there was a loud bang to my right. It was a gunshot. The sound of the glass from the kitchen window shattered into the sink below it.

Conor's smile was beginning to fade as blood began to fall out of a massive hole on the side of his head. His smoking hand slowly dropped, and his face fell onto the table.

Allen, who had been sprayed with Conor's blood, lowered his position to a tactical crouch. His rifle was no longer pointed at my chest but was instead aimed at the window, ready to react with fire.

A motorbike revved aggressively from outside while the sound of someone singing started. It was a lone, deep, bellowing voice singing the words to 'A dirty old town'. The same song that had been whistled down the phone to me hours before on my way here. The same song that was whistled down the phone to me years ago, that morning in my flat before all the real trouble started. I knew who it was. Better late than never, I thought to myself. There was still a hope of saving my little girl.

Mona had crouched her position, too. Her eyes were wide like a deer in the headlights as she gripped hard onto her pistol, not knowing where to point or how to react. She was terrified.

The revving of the motorbike got louder and more frequent. The singing continued. He was shouting out the words.

'Dirty old town, dirty old town!' the voice sang out.

Once the verse was complete, a riderless motorbike burst through the front door and crashed into the kitchen.

All three of us had just managed to dive to safety before it hit the table. Smoke came out of the engine as the bike fell to the ground. It was lying on top of Cara's ankles.

More gunfire came through the windows. When I looked up from the floor, Allen had grabbed Mona by the arm. They escaped through the back kitchen door, out into the night.

I had landed next to the top half of Cara's body. She was lying on her front with her left cheek to the ground. I looked down and, for a moment, stared into her sad-looking face. I was so angry with her, but it was Cara, she was my family...

I looked up at the kitchen door. The smell of the motorbike's engine was pungent in the air. Standing at the entrance, with a smoking rifle in his hand, was Rex."

Chapter Ten

"It was 2013 when I met Mindy for the first time.

I'd been in Camden for the day, drinking in the sun with a few of my army mates. I went out the back for a cigarette. Looking around, smoky smiles and ecliptic eyes painted the escapism of the weekend's ignorance to the pressures of the working week gone by.

It was Cara I spoke to first—a beautiful brunette who was standing alone outside in the outdated smoking area. I didn't approach her. I turned around, and she was there. Dressed in black. Arms and legs out. A vision of felicity as she unknowingly initiated my future while sipping on a cocktail through a plastic straw.

The sound of The Rolling Stones came from inside the bar, where IPA-drinking bearded men and gaggles of gorgeous young women laughed and howled as their honesty lost all filtration and an uncommon infatuation grew for one another with each drink.

Cara was pretty. She wasn't short but wasn't as tall as me, not even with her heels. A lot of time had been spent that day in front of the mirror with various brushes and products to cheat the city's eyes from the reality of her true reflection. Though she really didn't need all that makeup.

Her hair curled unnaturally in big waves of finessed beauty. Silver jewellery sparkled around her neck and wrists and hung from her ears. Her perfume was overpowering. It wasn't a terrible smell, but she didn't need the additional seven sprays. She was out to impress. She was a predator on the hunt for lustful arms, and her odds were favourable.

After around ten minutes, Mindy came looking for her friend. I was instantly enchanted, struck and hooked by her undertone. Though she seemed remarkably unimpressed by me. Mindy barely acknowledged my direction. She was the opposite of Cara, who was butter in my hands, giggling at my doltish stories and gently slapping and tugging at my arm with hopeful eyes.

Mindy, however, was reluctant of laughter. She was covered up, both emotionally and physically. Tight denim blue jeans fabricated her long, shapely legs. A pair of red high heels brought her expensive-looking sunglasses to my eye level. A slightly unbuttoned, baggy Ralph Lauren white shirt fell from her shoulders, half tucked into her waist. Long, straight copper-red hair was finger-combed over her head and away from her face every other minute, and a thin golden chain with a heart on the end fell from her neck. She smelled amazing, too. She effortlessly impressed. No one in the bar compared to her.

Cara proposed that we get a table outside. Mindy begrudgingly accepted and sat opposite me, chain-smoking in the sun while Cara and I nonsensically joked around and shot the shit. The only animation from Mindy came from the reflection in her sunglasses. She fiddled with her hair, twirling the ends around the fingers of her non-smoking hand. Bemused and soberly concentrated.

It wasn't until around twenty minutes later, when Cara went to the toilet, that Mindy finally spoke. For a moment, she didn't say a word. I'd run out of cigarettes. I asked her if I could have one of hers and got no reply. Instead, she just silently looked through me in an unbroken gaze of disappointment. If it wasn't for her smoking, you might have thought someone had pressed pause on a tele remote. There was no change in her frozen, emotionless state—just a continuous statue-like stare in my direction while I sipped on my mostly drunk flat lager.

Looking at my reflection in her sunglasses, I slowly reached for her pack of smokes, which lay in front of her on the table. Just as my hand got near enough to touch the pack, she quickly grabbed her lighter from next to it and lit it to burn my fingers. I pulled away quickly. Still, she refrained from emotion as she lay her lighter back down on the table.

'That was rude. Don't steal.' she said calmly before taking another drag of her cigarette. She had the sweetest-sounding voice. It was clear and almost tuneful.

'You burnt me.' I replied while rubbing the tips of my fingers. The burn didn't hurt; I just wanted to make it look like it did to see if I could trigger a reaction from her.

Mindy took a cigarette from the pack and put it between her juicy red lips. She then lit it, took a drag, and handed it to me. She was effortlessly cool, like a film star—radiant and well-postured, elegant and calm in her fluidity.

'Thanks.' I said. She didn't reply, though she was still looking at me.

'Where's that accent from?' I asked.

'I don't have an accent. I sound literally the same as you.' she replied.

'Well, that's not true. We all have an accent. And you seem to be… lavishly well-spoken.' She didn't reply.

'Dad rich?' I asked.

'Why?'

'You just give off that vibe.' I proclaimed boldly, with the kind of confidence a few pints of lager can bring.

'And what vibe is that?'

'Well, your threads are beautiful. Simple. They look expensive and new, suggesting you don't need to parade your wealth about; that novelty surrounding the notion of brandishing your fortunate hand has long passed and is now beneath interest. You're without a wedding ring, and you're too young to have a job that can afford both your style and the rent in the city. Also, your watch says Chanel on it.'

'I don't live in the city. And maybe I know the places to shop which are good value for money. Maybe my watch is fake?'

'Is it fake?'

'I doubt it. Dad bought it for me.'

'What's your dad do?'

"That's none of your business.'

'Do you have a boyfriend?'

'That's none of your business.'

'Girlfriend?'

'No. You?'

'That's none of your business.' I said. Mindy shook her head slightly. She wasn't impressed.

'What do you do for work?' I asked.

'I'm a model, but I don't like it. You?'

'I'm in the Parachute Regiment.'

'As in the army?'

'As in the army. Why don't you like modelling?'

'I'm bored of it. Standing around all day.'

'What do you want to do instead?'

'I'd like to be a writer.'

'You could be and do both? No? A writer of what sorts?'

'Fiction.'

'I'll buy your book.'

'You don't know what it's about. Also, I only have the scraps of ideas at the minute.'

'I'll still read it. I like to read. You could write one about a supermodel who meets a Para? Can you take your sunglasses off?'

'Why do you want me to take my glasses off?' she replied in a dulcet tone.

'I just want to see something'.

There was a brief pause.

'No.' she said confidently and continued to smoke.

'Why not?' I said provocatively, as if she might have something to hide.

'Take yours off.'

'Bit forward, we've just met. And who says I'm wearing anyway?'

'Ha, ha… Take your glasses off.' she said, unimpressed.

I took my glasses off, folded them up and put them on the table in front of me. Mindy didn't take hers off. She just kept staring at me while slowly smoking.

I smiled and raised an eyebrow to hint that it was her turn, but still, she didn't move. So I rested my burning cigarette in the ashtray in the middle of us both and slowly reached out to put my hands on either side of her face. Then, I carefully pulled her glasses off.

I wasn't sure what I was expecting to see, but I wasn't expecting that. She was gorgeous—truly stunning, effortlessly enriched in charm.

I examined her face. She had pale white skin and bright, icy-blue eyes. Her makeup was minimal, yet her lashes were full and long, and her eyebrows were softly angled; they were sisters but not twins in their symmetry. A small, thin, perfect nose sat above her big red heart-shaped lips. Her face was thin, soft, radiant and perfectly in proportion. It was her eyes that blew me away the most. They had a look of seduction, strength and vulnerability all mixed together.

'Why would you hide them?' I asked.

'What are you talking about?' she replied in a repulsed tone as if offended.

'Your eyes. They're beautiful.'

For a split second, she smiled. A slight dimple formed on the side of her mouth on her perfectly sculpted face before it transformed into disgust.

'That was awful. Borderline disgusting. Do these lines normally work for you?' she asked.

'It wasn't a line. You're beautiful.'

'Stop. I think I'm gonna be sick. That was pathetic. Stop saying that, or I might actually throw up in your beer.'

'What? It's not a line; I'm just saying. You've obviously seen yourself. It can't be a fucking... shock to you? You're a model. I've not said you're fit or hot. You surpass that.'

'You're a fucking nerd.' she said assertively. I laughed.

'No, I'm not. I've just not met many people as pretty as you. Well, not in a long time anyway.' It was true. She was the only woman I'd met who was anywhere near Mona in terms of beauty. She didn't reply instantly; she just continued to smoke and sipped on her drink through a plastic straw.

'Thanks. I guess you're pretty, too. Even if your jokes are shit. I wasn't sure what to expect before you took your glasses off either, and truthfully, I didn't really care. But it was a… pleasant surprise, I suppose. But don't get the wrong idea, Jake. Once Cara's back, we're leaving, and you'll have to find someone else to try your luck with.'

'Jack.'

'What?'

'My name is Jack. Not Jake.'

'I don't care.'

'What's your name? I know it's Mindy, but what's Your full name?'

'Why? Gonna stalk me online? Knew you was a weirdo.'

'No, I don't have social media. What's your name?'

'Why would you not?... It's Madeline. Mindy Madeline'

'I knew I knew you?'

'What?'

'I've seen some of your films.'

'What films?'

'You do those intense artistic, adult movies?'

'What? What do you… no. No, I do not do porn.'

'Well you've a name like a bloody Porn star.'

'That's rude. I really don't like you.'

'Sorry. I'm only joking. Let me buy you a drink as an apology. I'll go and order a couple of cocktails… Porn star martinis?'

Mindy scowled at me.

'What's your name?' she asked.

'Why? Are you gonna stalk me online?'

'Don't be a dick, Jake; you've just told me you don't have any social media. Which is really fucking weird. What is it?'

'Jack.'

'Jack, Jake, Whatever. What's your surname?'

'Duke. Jackson Duke.'

'Jackson Duke? Are you fucking joking? That's hilarious. Sounds like a bloody dog's name. Duke? Jesus.' she said while laughing softly to herself. Her laugh was heavenly.

'I wouldn't mock if I were you, could be your surname one day.' I said while docking out the end of my cigarette in the ashtray.

'No chance. Hell would have to freeze over before that happened. You're pretty and everything, but I'm not into you. Sorry. You're not my type. It's what you say. You've barely said anything... meaningful or with any substance since we met. Just shit joke after shit joke.'

'Well, imagine the audacity of lowering the tone on this beautiful day of communal escapism to divert the attention of harmonious laughter towards the solemn discussions of Marxists, politics, economic disorder, or whether there is a triumph in the believing or denying the belief of an omnipotent spiritual force that truly rules over all creatures great and tiny... anyway, Cara thinks I'm funny.'

'Well, why don't you go and fuck her then?'

'Maybe I will.'

'Okay.'

'Okay.'

'Okay...' she said bitterly.

Then Cara came back from the toilet. Neither Mindy or I looked at her as she sat down. We were too busy looking at each other.

'Anyone want another drink?' Cara asked.

'I'll get them. I owe Miss Madeline a Porn star martini.'

Mindy laughed slightly under her breath.

'We need to get going to the Blues Kitchen, Cara. That band you wanted to see will be on soon. Jackson Duke… you coming?' Mindy asked.

'I thought I wasn't to see you again?'

'I'm not gonna ask twice.' Mindy said assertively while putting her sunglasses back on as she stood up to leave. I got up too and quickly texted my mate Jason Frost that I was getting off and would see him and the boys later on.

At the next bar, we drank and danced into the morning, getting more and more drunk by the hour. Then, at some point after two o'clock, we headed back to their hotel room with three bottles of wine.

Between us, we finished one of the bottles in the back of a taxi. We stumbled through the hotel corridors, laughing and shouting along the way. Then, in the hotel room, suddenly, everyone was kissing each other. Clothes were being ripped off, and wine was being poured into each other's mouths while the sound of the early, early morning radio show played chilled dance tracks from a television in the background.

I was later told that neither of the girls had ever done anything like that before. In fact, Mindy said she had only slept with three other people before that night. She had a long-term boyfriend from school who she split up with a couple of years ago when she was twenty-two. Then, to get over him, she had a drunken one-night stand. She also had a small fling with a model, but that had ended a few months back.

After over an hour of steamy, drunken sex, Mindy put her shirt on and went over to the window to smoke. I put my boxer shorts on and joined her. She looked happy. A lot happier than when we first met. We talked, not really about anything, but it flowed so naturally. More naturally than it had with anyone before. There weren't any bullshit jokes either, yet I was making her laugh, and a lot too.

She told me she'd read about people like me. I said that was bollocks. Absurd. However, she insisted.

'I have. I've read about the Parachute Regiment. You boys are crazy. You've conquered fear, they say.' she said.

'We've given it a good go, but there aren't many that are truly free of fear. Courage is to feel the fear and to do it anyway. Reward often only comes from risk.'

Then Mindy leant forward and kissed me. It was a different kind of kiss to the one that had happened between us before when Cara was involved. Her lips were vigorous and passionate as they met mine.

'What was that for?' I asked when it ended.

'I'd been wanting to do it all night, but I was scared. So I felt the fear and did it anyway.' she replied softly while looking into my eyes.

Cara was lying naked, fast asleep on the bed. Mindy pulled the quilt cover over her, and then we both sat on the floor and shared the last bottle of wine while talking and laughing quietly for hours.

We had a lot in common. We shared the same sense of humour and admiration for making light of the topics that weren't necessarily politically correct. We both loved wine, particularly red. Mindy played the piano very well, and I played the guitar. She found it amusing when I told her that I thought the relationship for the interval between the likes of G and E minor worked so well was because they were just really good mates, and to learn that they were, in fact, related blew my mind. She also found it amusing that I could only play the piano in the key of C.

The main differences that stood out were our upbringings. Mindy was very wealthy and middle class. She had never taken any drugs and didn't have a drop of alcohol until her eighteenth birthday. I loved that. Her teen years were spent with her head in a book and working hard on schoolwork. She was never particularly rebellious at all.

Although I hadn't done any drugs since joining the army, I had done a lot in my late teens and early twenties. I barely spent a day sober. And I grew up incredibly poor and working class, and I fucked about at every chance that I could.

We were from different worlds. She had a dishwasher, and I didn't really know what one was. She had been skiing as a child each year, and I had been once with the army, and I had never been out of the UK before I enlisted. Her education was paid for; my school shoes had holes in them most of the time. Yet we clicked. And it turned out that she had found me a lot funnier than she had let on to back at the first bar.

When Cara woke Mindy up the next morning by running to the toilet to be sick, we were asleep on the floor in each other's arms. Mindy was smiling as she woke me with a kiss on the cheek. Her doting eyes met mine. She kissed me again and then cuddled her head around my neck, squeezing me tightly with her arms.

After that night, I saw Mindy every weekend and any chance possible in between, unless I was away on exercise with the army. We became obsessed with each other and quickly became an item.

The sex was crazy. It felt like so much more than with anyone I'd slept with before. I was falling in love, and that didn't scare me. I was in awe of her.

That was out of character for me. I hadn't been in a relationship since Mona. It felt so different from when I was with Mona. Everything felt like so much more—the conversation, connection, laughter, and playfulness. Everything was heightened.

I talked to Mindy on the phone daily. All I thought about was her. I was desperate to spend more time with her. The mental thing was that she felt exactly the same about me.

Mindy was the smartest person I knew. She changed my whole perspective on everything. I wasn't unhappy before we met. I was having a great time surrounded by my mates in army life. But meeting her was like seeing life through a new lens. She was classy and proper, sophisticated and cultured. A lover of animals, nature and how things worked. She read everything. Whenever we spoke on the phone, her head was either in a book or an article. And though she was accustomed to the finer things in life, she was incredibly appreciative of the small.

It was hard for Mindy when she learned a few months after that night in London that Cara had fallen pregnant with my child. She was heartbroken that it wasn't her instead. So I got down on one knee and proposed. It felt like the best thing to do. I didn't want to lose her, ever. I wanted her to know how devoted I was to her and only her.

I told Mindy I would leave the army to be with her more and that I was going to go into business with Rex. To begin with, I didn't tell her what the business was, though she assumed after meeting Rex for the first time that it wasn't kosher. She'd never met anyone like him. I told her before the wedding what the true nature of the business was. She weirdly didn't mind. 'No risk, no reward.' she said. However, she was very concerned about it all ending badly.

I never told Cara about my business with Rex. She was in the dark about the whole thing, and thought I did something on the computer to do with sales and data analysis for work. I also told Cara that Rex was just an old army mate of mine. I downplayed my relationship with him completely to her so that she'd ask fewer questions. The less she knew, the better. It was for the best, just in case the whole thing went sideways and the law came knocking one day. That way, she couldn't accidentally drop me in it or get excited and tell someone too much if she was drunk one night.

The wedding day was monumental. Fucking hell. It was a day that I never imagined my wedding to have looked like. It must have cost a fortune. The venue was stunning.

The food was extraordinary. There was a delicate attention to detail in every avenue of wonder that I would never have thought of. From the seating arrangements to the invitations, the timings and the cake. What people were fucking wearing. Everything was staggeringly startling.

Mindy's mum loved me, but her dad wasn't as keen. He was unimpressed that he had to pay for a wedding where his only daughter's maid of honour was the mother of the groom's child. You could hardly blame him. But they both knew how much we loved each other.

Mindy looked so beautiful in that white dress. Stunning. She looked so sure and happy walking down that aisle, floating and eager to be my wife. When it was time to kiss the bride, she kissed me harder than she ever had before.

At the reception, we barely left each other's side. Our hands or arms were constantly intertwined. Afterwards, I didn't know whether it was rude or not to pay such little attention to the guests. But I didn't care. I just wanted to be with Mrs Mindy Duke.

Mindy mostly invited the people there that day. I just had a few army mates and Rex, of course.

Jason Frost was my best man and Isla's godfather. Rex was her second godfather. Both stood at the altar with me.

I went through basic training with Jason Frost. Then we were both in 2 Para together. He was a tall and well-built black man from St Lucia. Jason was a year younger than me, but you would have thought he was older. He had moved over to the UK just to join the elite fighting force. It took him a long time to adapt to the British weather, especially the snow, which I found hilarious. He was so excited when he saw it for the first time. I'd never seen anyone run back indoors so quickly as he did when he discovered that it was cold as fuck. He was so pissed off.

If it wasn't for Jason, I maybe wouldn't have made it through the Parachute Regiment training programme. We supported each other completely in the hard times. I could rely on him for anything. We always found laughter in the face of adversity. There were countless times that we were both sat in the pouring rain, freezing our feet off, and covered in bangs and bruises with different pains coming from different parts of our exhausted bodies, laughing and joking instead of moaning and complaining like some of the others… like Allen. His positivity was infectious, much like Mindy's. I loved him like a brother. He was a real gentleman.

Jason stayed in the army when I left to work his way up through the ranks of the elite Regiment and try out for special forces selection. I was heartbroken to learn that he'd died in action a couple of years after the wedding. He was one of the bravest men I knew, both on the battlefield and the dancefloor.

Nine months after that night in London, Isla was born. My whole world changed. I couldn't believe how small her tiny little hands were. I loved her instantly. I didn't know it was possible to love something so much.

The four of us, Mindy, Cara, Isla, and myself, moved into our first house in Stamford. It was small—just a two-bedroom. I was still in the transition period of leaving the military for a few months, so I was back and forth a lot, but Cara had Mindy for support when I wasn't there.

Over a year later, we moved into the big house on the outskirts of Stamford. I had been working with Rex for a while, and the money was already rolling in fast.

I'd be lying if I said I didn't miss the army, but I wouldn't have changed a thing. Those years in Stamford were the happiest I'd ever been. It may seem like a weird setup, our family, but it didn't feel like that. It felt natural and effortless.

The house was huge. The girls chose and decorated the interior. Cara and Isla had their own bedrooms. Isla even had her own separate playroom. There were two living rooms, but we only ever used one. The other Mindy would read and write in.

We spent a lot of time drinking wine in the kitchen in the evenings. It had a lengthy dining table at the back that led onto the patio doors leading to the garden.

We occasionally had people round for a barbecue, either the girl's friends from school or, a couple of times, my mates from the army. Often, Rex would be there if he was in the area. Most of the time, it would just be the four of us.

The girls and I would all holiday somewhere sunny together at least twice a year, though Mindy and I went away on our own a lot for just the weekend.

Mindy wanted to wait a few years to have kids. She didn't want to take the spotlight away from Isla. She adored being Isla's stepmum and was anxious about how Cara would feel and adapt to her falling pregnant.

Cara was already a bit of an emotional wreck. If it wasn't for the support of Mindy being there for her then she'd likely have toppled over the edge.

Cara kept her true feelings for me well hidden. From the morning after that night in London, she was adamant that she wasn't interested or bothered by the connection between Mindy and me. She said she had seen it from the start. Our relationship, to me, felt like what I imagined having a sibling would be like. Or maybe Mindy and I were too caught up in each other to notice her properly.

The girls didn't need to work. They both quit their jobs and stayed home to look after Isla. Mindy spent a lot of her days reading and writing. Cara would watch daytime television while recovering from a hangover. She always drank a bit too much after Mindy and I had gone to bed.

In the week, I often drove up and down the country to meet with Rex. Sometimes, we'd have to do trips abroad, which usually turned into a bit of a jolly and involved a lot of drinking once the job was done.

Several times, I had to parachute down with the contraband to deliver the weapons if we couldn't find a safe route by road. I fucking loved doing it that way.

We had a good system to avoid being caught. Rex was a very careful and calculated man. He had friends and connections who would help us with fake documentation and identification or renting vehicles and properties.

My daughter, Isla, was dreamy from day one. She was absolutely beautiful, always was. I loved nothing more in the world, and she loved her dad in equal measure. Everyone always told us that she was an angel with a heart of gold. I didn't need telling, I knew.

I would play with her every evening until she got too tired, and I would read to her to sleep at night. Weirdly, she was more interested in playing with soldiers than dolls. I didn't mind. In fact, I loved it. I tried to teach her everything I knew.

Mindy had taught her to read; by age four, she was already pretty good. My favourite sound in the world was hearing Isla read me a story. It was so clear, sweet, and oddly very posh. She must have gotten that voice from the girls.

Isla was always very sassy and confident but in a charming and adorable way. She had her mother's dark hair—long locks that she was obsessed with brushing all the time—copying the girls.

When she started school, I would pick her up afterwards, and she would sprint into my arms when she saw me and give me the biggest hug ever.

I got her to start taking kickboxing lessons at the age of five, too, and she also got really good at that. She was so strong for such a young girl and had a hell of a punch on her.

Isla was unusually smart for a seven-year-old. Her teachers at school were all wonderstruck by how advanced her intellectual development was. She carried herself and spoke like a child a couple of years senior her age. Her learning surpassed the other children in her class as she dazzled in each subject, especially Maths, English and Science. It made it hard for her to make friends with the other kids, but it didn't seem to bother her too much. I was worried about her, though. I wanted her to have all the friends in the world and to play and laugh instead of sitting alone reading at lunchtime.

I'd had four best friends in my life up to that point. That's if you don't count, Isla. Isla was my number one. Rex was up there, too, I guess, but he was more like a father figure. But my four best friends were Mo, Mona, Jason Frost, and Mindy. I loved all of them, but without a doubt, Mindy was my soul mate. I was so in love with her. We never argued; we just made each other's lives easier. She'd wake up with the most beautiful smile, full of excitement for the day ahead. And she wouldn't fall asleep until we'd shown each other just how much we loved one another.

My wife had a talent for turning everyone's darkest hours into the brightest moments. She gave everyone the time and attention they needed to feel heard and appreciated. Everyone loved and adored her. I was completely obsessed with her. We were obsessed with each other."

Chapter Eleven

"I was devasted the night Mindy died.

I had been overtaking cars on the motorway for nearly two hours, passing them by and leaving them out of reach until their headlights were like forgotten stars in my mirrors. It was after four in the morning. Rex was beside me, smoking in the passenger seat with the window ajar, fiddling with the radio to find a song he liked while we sped towards his city, Manchester.

Rex had aged well for someone who had the lungs of a chimney. He was still in incredible shape. Muscular and lean, and maybe a stone heavier than what he had weighed in his mid-thirties. A couple of new tattoos had been inked into his skin. His big ginger moustache, like always, was perfectly crafted below his smooth bald head. The lines on his face cut deeper with age, though they only enriched his rugged good looks. However, his aggressive nature was still terrifying to look upon, maybe more so.

Allen and Mona managed to escape in one of the cars parked outside the front of the house just after Rex's riderless motorbike crashed through the front door. Rex sprinted outside when he heard their engine start. He fired his rifle at the back of the car as they raced away from the scene. None of the shots managed to stop them.

His motorbike wasn't in a good way. Black smoke floated aloft to the kitchen ceiling, but we didn't have the time to acknowledge it properly.

Not long after the pair of them got away, Conor's phone started to ring. I searched the dead man's pockets. His body was in a heap on the floor to the side of the table. A pool of blood from his head had formed a puddle that would soon converge with Cara's.

I answered his phone. A voice I recognised was on the other end. She sounded nervous and scared and was struggling to speak. It was Mona.

'Jack. You know where to go, Jack. Where it all began, where you killed him, hurry. I'm not the only one who's missing Daddy.' she said quietly in a mouselike whisper before hanging up.

'The yard.' I told Rex.

'What you talking about, ya pervert?' he said while standing over Cara's bleeding body, observing and shaming her. Her eyes were still open. A frozen and haunted look of desperation stared back at him.

'She's being taunted by fire, that one. I can see it in her eyes. A hellish anguish. Eternally damned. Her soul is well and truly fucked, mate.' said Rex in his bellowing voice.

'It was Mona. On the phone. Isla's, at the O'Brien's yard. We have to get there now!'

'Then what are we still doing here? Grab that dead pervert's keys. Nick his ciggies, too, and see if he's got any petrol money. I'll be having that lighter as well, the gold one.' Rex said before storming outside. The heavy sound of his boots hammered into the ground as his giant, bloodied footprints left a trail from the murderous scene.

I found Conor's keys in his other pocket and took ninety pounds out of his wallet. I left his cigarettes; they were soaked in his blood. I took his golden lighter, engraved with 'O'Brien'. I wiped it on my river-soaked jeans and put it in my pocket.

I didn't know what they had done with my stuff. My phone, my keys, my rifle. But there wasn't the time to look for them. We had a long drive ahead of us, and the hour was already far from being a friend.

When I got outside, Rex was walking towards me with a large black bergen over his shoulder and a motorbike helmet in his hand.

I pressed the keys' unlock button, and the lights of a

black Range Rover flashed in front of us. Rex took off his leather jacket, and we climbed in and drove off into the night towards another Mancunian morning.

The drive from Stamford to Manchester took about three hours, and I had to try to shorten it as much as possible.

'It's fucking lucky I was still in Nottingham, or I would never of gotten to you, not until it was too late anyway. You would of been brown fucking bread, mate, truly.' said Rex while we sped along the motorway.

'Fourteen fucking years, I've been wanting to know who that whistler was. It was you the whole time… Jesus… what took you so long to call me back anyway? And why was your number withheld?'

'Ahh, I missed your call because I was enjoying the company of a lovely young lady called Sarah… or was it, Sara?... Anyway, nice bird. Smashing pair.'

'Right... Why was your phone withheld?'

'Well, because you, you little pervert, rang me at an ungodly hour, and I wanted to freak you the fuck out on account of disrupting my champagned bubbled bath with the lovely Sarah… or Sara.'

'Where'd you get the rifle from?'

'I brought it down with me in my overnight bag. Stayed over in Notts at a hotel didn't I the night before we met yesterday. Always have one on me when we meet someone about a deal, just in case some pervert wants to get a bit lively and kicks off. The birds fucking love it too. Really gets them going.' he said while twizzling and curling the ends of his ginger moustache in the sun mirror.

'Right.' I replied sarcastically. There was no room for humour, and there wouldn't be until my little girl was safe again and back with me.

'Don't worry, Jack, we'll get Isla. And we'll get those perverts that took her and did that to R' Mindy. God rest her soul. Fucking shocking. Criminal what Cara did, absolutely criminal.'

'Rex... you sell guns and drugs for a living.'

'Yeah, well... I still have my fucking morals. I am simply a man of business, mate. That is all. And when the time comes, I will be welcomed by your dearly beloved at the gates of heaven, where Christ himself will offer me a cold beer and a firm shake of the hand. I've a promising intuition that Jesus and I will be the firmest of friends.'

'Right...' I said again sarcastically. I still hadn't processed that Mindy was really dead. Rex saying it aloud hit me like a steamroller, flattening my spirit and rolling out my heartache across a world where no hope lived. It started to sink in like a ship hitting the seabed. I realised she was gone. A teardrop fell down my cheek. I wiped it quickly, hoping that Rex hadn't seen.

'Jack, have a ciggie mate. Now's not the time for that. You can grieve when this is all over and Isla's back home. Right now, we have to be focused and fucking ferocious. We've got a thunderous storm awaiting us. We don't know the kind of numbers we're up against, and they'll be expecting us. I'll make a few phone calls, see what I can get sorted, but I need to try and get it done with as few knowing as possible. There's a truce in the city between my lot and the O'Brien's and a few other perverts, too. And I'm about to break that truce. If word gets out, there'll be an almighty war. It'll be like a fucking cowboy movie, mate. I do actually know a geezer who's got a horse, too.'

'I know. We need a plan, though. How are we going to get in? We'll be walking right into another trap.'

'What you need is clean socks, coffee and calories. Pull over at the next services.'

'Rex, we don't have time for that.'

'Proper preparation prevents piss poor performance. You should know that. You're ex-Reg. That's what they taught us when I tried out for the Paras.'

'You've never mentioned this before.'

'Ahh, I didn't do very long. A few weeks. I didn't get a

big enough hard-on over it all to withstand the suffering of nature.'

'What?... You didn't like the wet and cold?'

'Not one fucking bit. Hated it. Fucking lying in a puddle all day while the rain pisses down on you and some geezers shouting a world of pain in your face. Fuck that. But I'm very proud of what you've achieved and the man you've grown to be. You've surrounded the storm of pain and fought through to become victor of both the mind and the body. Very proud I am. But, even if you are resilient enough to fight on an empty stomach, I, my friend, am not. Could do with a bit of petrol, too.'

Rex was right; we needed petrol. I pulled over a few miles later at the next services and filled the car up while Rex went inside to pay with Conor O'Brien's cash. When he came back, he had two black coffees, four bottles of water, six flapjacks, four Snickers bars, and a pair of pink socks.

We swapped places. I sat in the passenger seat and changed out of my wet socks into the new pink ones while Rex drove north.

'Where these the only colour?' I asked. Rex laughed.

'No. I got them for my own amusement. And I thought, Isla, would like seeing you wear them too... Did Cara say why she did it?'

'Apparently, she was in love with me and had been all along. So she said anyway. Was news to me. Mindy had no idea, either. She was a bit troubled, Cara. Not very good with her head. She got hold of Mona, thinking that she and Isla would be left with the money once Mindy and I were out the way.'

'A bit troubled? That's a way to put it. She were fucking mental. She had that look about her. A killer's eyes. Pretty, but a messed-up piece to the puzzle. Only took a couple glasses of wine for the crazy to blossom into a demonic dance of witchlike wilding worry. She'd willingly drown a fucking bubble that one. I've always known it. To me, people are windows. And through her window was a godforsaken garden of raging desperation, spinning the dice on a thirst for what is truly unholy, mate.'

'Right…' I replied, again sarcastically.

Rex got word from Michael, one of his men, that he had watching the O'Brien's yard. He said there was movement going on within the office. He just saw a man and a woman go inside, and it looked like a couple of others were in there, too, but he couldn't work out how many, though he assumed no more than six.

'The geezer who's just gone in had a mega piece on him too, G. Big old boy. Aint fucking about. The front gates be open too.' said Michael, he was on loudspeaker on Rex's phone.

'What about the bird?' asked Rex.

'Couldn't really see Rex. Looked a real ting though, still.'

'Are there any perverts on the front gate?'

'Na, man. There be no brothers there. Fucking hell, though, man; someone looks pretty mad, though, innit. I think he just flipped a desk. Can hear a bit of shouting. I'll send you a video, still.'

'Good man, Michael. Stay tight. I'll call you when I'm nearly there.'

'Bless G, bless.' Michael said before Rex ended the call.

Moments later, Michael sent Rex a video. He had zoomed in on the windows. I could see Liam O'Brien pacing around, looking very distressed. Mona walked past the window, too.

'One thing we do have to our advantage is that we have that dead pervert's keys. They'll open the back gate if we need to get in that way.' said Rex as he swerved in and out of the cars on the now slightly busier motorway. That got me thinking. They were sitting ducks in the middle of the yard.

'We need a distraction, a diversion, and some sort of element of surprise.' I said.

'I think I have an idea.' said Rex confidently before lighting a cigarette.

We arrived at Manchester. That wasn't my first time back in the city. I'd been back many times, but the nostalgia still hit me like it always did as we drove along the lit-up city roads. The air was different there than to down south. It had a bite to it. There was always the scent of something about to happen, a smell that anything could happen.

Mo was laughing and joking in my memory, and I remembered all the times Mona and I had driven along the familiar route, hand in hand like love-struck teenagers, thinking we were the only ones who mattered. I hadn't seen or heard from Katie since the day Mo died. I wondered if Mona had ever told her what happened. Were they even still friends?

'We'll make a quick stop off at mine, get what we need.' said Rex, exhaling cigarette smoke.

Rex had a big three-bedroom house in Chorlton, Manchester. His old school Land Rover and big white transit van were in the driveway out the front. We parked up further down the road and went inside.

I knew the house well. The only times I had been back to the city were to drop off or pick something up, usually guns or money.

From the inside, the house didn't look like what you'd expect of a notorious gangster. There were plants everywhere and a vast amount of different styled armchairs in each room, most with a small table to their side with an empty ashtray on top. The house was unusually clean, but that wasn't from Rex's doing, he had a cleaner go round twice a week.

Rex told me he'd meet me in the living room, which was the first room on the right down the hall. I went in and lit a cigarette while impatiently pacing around the room, nervously imagining different scenarios of how the rest of the day might have panned out. I was desperate for Isla to be safe and to remain safe. Nothing else mattered.

Rex's living room was large. It had been painted dark red but had a cream-coloured ceiling and skirting board with a dark red carpet. A snooker table sat in the middle. There was no television, that was in the kitchen. Two armchairs sat close to the curtain-closed window, both angled in to face the centre of the room. A small table was between them with an ashtray on top. The curtains were that same shade of dark red.

On the other side of the room was a bar with four stools lined up along it. An assortment of different spirits and liquors were on the bar, and a cabinet was to its side that held a variety of different-sized glasses. Behind the bar was a mini fridge that I knew was stocked with bottles of beer and fruit juices. A large stereo system was sat on a cupboard in the other corner to the left.

A fireplace was in the middle of the long wall, behind the snooker table and opposite the door. It had a huge mirror hanging above it.

An array of plants finessed the space. Some were on top of the fireplace, one was on the bar, two were on a table by the door where another ashtray was, and there was a thin mini tree in the corner of the room to the right of the window.

Framed photographs of Manchester United and various photographs of Rex with people at his bar throughout the years were hung around the walls.

Rex walked into the room a few minutes later with a giant gym bag. He dropped the bag on top of the snooker table. The sound of metal clanked together as it hit the surface.

'Toys, mate.' he said while pulling out a cigarette from a packet in his jeans. The bag was full of guns, ammunition and other tools that we would find useful for the task ahead."

Chapter Twelve

The cigar-smoking man put his hand up and smiled.

"Jack, I think you'll be interested in hearing this.

Inside the O'Brien's yard, the death of Connor was being angrily mourned by the two remaining brothers. Liam and Paddy Wang had just learned on Mona and Allen's arrival that their eldest brother, and their leader, had been killed by an unknown accomplice of yours.

Liam flipped a desk over in a rage while swearing at the top of his voice. The deep and bellowing profanity terrified Isla, who was sitting on the floor in the far corner of the room, barefoot and cold. She wasn't crying and did her best not to look as scared as she felt. She stayed quiet while observing and listening to her kidnappers.

It was Hector, one of the O'Brien's men, who had stolen her. He had taken her in her sleep and locked her in the back of a van. Then he drove her north to the yard.

Earlier that night, Isla went to bed as normal, with her mother and Mindy wishing her the sweetest of dreams with a kiss on the forehead. That was the last thing she knew until she woke up in the O'Brien's office. Cara had secretly given Isla a sedative before she went to sleep so she would know less of the night. The plan was for Cara to be there in the yard before Isla woke up. However, Mona didn't keep to the plan, and Isla was terrified.

The two brothers and Hector had been there the whole time with Isla. Paddy Wang hadn't moved from his chair as he sat chain-smoking weed at his desk. Liam had switched between pacing up and down to sitting at the desk his father used to work from in the opposite corner to where Isla was. Hector had taken the chair from Liam's workspace and was sat by Conor's desk next to Liam.

Time had been cruel to all three men. The brothers were both in their late forties, though Liam looked a lot older and had put on a stone in fat. Paddy Wang was still immaculately presented in a smartly ironed shirt and trousers. His heavy cocaine use had taken the life from his eyes, as with Liam. The little man's side-parted hair was still styled perfectly, but a dull shade of aged grey had been peppered into it.

Hector, the family's most loyal worker, was a skinny, skeletal man in his sixties with a grey goatee and slicked-back grey hair. He had dirt behind his fingernails, his skin was wrinkled and weathered, and he smelled like a bonfire in a brothel.

Hector and Liam were in Jeans, which was a rarity for Liam. Hector wore an old, dirty-looking checked shirt, while Liam wore a black Stone Island jumper with a golden chain hanging from his neck. Liam's effort to dress up was for Cara's benefit. He'd been looking forward to meeting her after Mona showed him a photograph from her Facebook.

All the desks had Mac computers, apart from Big Paddy's, which had become the only one without a computer and was instead used to hold paperwork and car magazines.

Aside from a framed photograph of Big Paddy on the wall and an upgraded coffee machine, the office hadn't changed at all in fourteen years. The walls were the same, just dirtier and more smoke-stained. The same was true of the carpet, though a lady did hoover, clean the toilet, change the bins, and wipe the surfaces and the window once a week.

Outside, there were just as many cars as the night Mo died—more, in fact. Business had been booming, both in their legal and illegal enterprises, as they profited greatly and their network soared.

Liam and Paddy Wang still shared an expensive city-centre flat and were both still without the love of a woman.

That is apart from their mother, Alannah, who lived in the same farmhouse as she did when her husband was alive.

Alannah was incredibly fit, healthy, and full of spirit for a woman in her late seventies. She enjoyed a life of blissful solitude on the farm, doing crosswords and reading books, though she adored nothing more than a call from a grandchild.

Two of Conor's three children were living away at university, while the youngest finished his A levels at a college in the city.

Conor's wife lived a life of unfulfilled misery as each day ended at the bottom of a bottle. None of them had anything to do with the family business. Conor wanted it that way. He didn't want to force his children into a life of corruption like his dad had forced him. He enjoyed the idea of his children living a normal life, away from crime and animosity.

'Who was the shooter?' Hector asked in a whiskey voice, just after the room had settled from Liam flipping over his dad's desk. Isla sat wide-eyed, hugging her legs tightly as her knees pressed against her chin. She was still in her matching pink pyjama set that she'd gone to bed in the night before.

'We didn't see him.' Mona admitted.

'What do you fucking mean you didn't see him!?' Liam asked angrily.

'The shot was fired through the window; then a motorbike crashed through the front door. We got out the back and drove here.' Johnny Allen replied.

'Well, who was on the motorbike?' asked Hector.

'No one. Just after Conor was shot, someone started revving the motorbike while singing.' said Allen. The two brothers and Hector looked at each other, confused.

'What? What kind of motorbike was it?' Liam asked aggressively.

'I'm not one hundred per cent, but it looked to be a Suzuki.' Allen guessed.

'What colour?' asked Hector.

'Black.' said Allen.

'What? What the fuck are you talking about? A riderless motorbike? And someone was singing a song? What fucking song?' Hector asked while Liam paced back and forth in a rage of anger.

'Dirty Old Town.' Mona said quietly.

Paddy Wang smacked his walking cane hard on his desk and looked at each adult in the room with a repulsed glare before returning to his brother's eyes.

'Rex.' Paddy Wang declared confidently.

'What? No, it can't be. He wouldn't have been able to get to Stamford from Manchester in time. I spoke to Rex a few years ago, too. He said he hadn't seen Jack since the night he left the city.' pleaded Mona.

'Fucking bullshit!' insisted Paddy Wang.

'Aye, it's Rex. That would explain a lot. That Cara bird did say, Jack, had a funny old mate from the army, a big geezer with a ginger tash that used to go round a couple times a year.' said Liam, nodding slowly with an evil glare.

'If only she was still around to ask her more.' Allen hinted at Mona's earlier outburst of emotion. Mona wasn't meant to shoot Cara; that wasn't part of the plan.

The men in the room started to suggest ideas on how to deal with the situation, such as burning down Rex's bar or slaughtering the men who worked for him.

Mona, however, had lost all interest in the matter. She had caught eyes with Isla for the first time. Mona's heart was enchanted with admiration. A maternal glow had gotten under her skin as a beautiful smile fused around her dimples. Isla saw and buried her little head within her shoulders to make herself as small as possible.

Mona slowly walked over to Isla, ignoring the ongoing conversation in the room, and knelt in front of the young girl.

'Hello.' Mona said to Isla in a friendly and warm tone.

'Hi.' Isla replied quietly in a shy little voice.

'My name's Mona.'

'My name's Isla.'

'That's a very pretty name. You have beautiful eyes; they're much like your dad's.'

'Thanks. I think your eyes are pretty, too.'

'Oh, Isla, thank you. How old are you?'

'Seven.'

'Adorable.' said Mona while smiling and shaking her head.

'How do you know my dad?'

'Your dad and I… your dad and I were friends. Best friends. A long time ago.'

'Were you his girlfriend?'

'Yes, yes I was.'

'Do you know my mum?'

'A little bit.'

'Can I see her?'

Mona paused and reached out to play with the ends of the young girl's hair.

'Your hair, it's beautiful. You're a very pretty girl.'

'You're avoiding the question and distracting me with charm.'

Mona giggled; she had an instant affection for Isla.

'You're a bright little thing, aren't you?' said Mona.

'My grades are the best in my class. Can I see my mum, please? Or Mindy?'

Mona paused and looked Isla in the eyes.

'Isla… I'm afraid your mum can't come. Your mum, she… well, she died a few hours ago.'

Isla's eyes started to water, and her breathing began to change.

'Don't cry, baby girl. It's okay.' Mona said while wiping away the tears on the little girl's cheek.

'Where's my dad?'

'Your dad should be here soon.'

'Where's Mindy?'

Mona paused and looked to her side to hide the distress of knowing that Mindy was your wife and not her. A tear fell down Mona's face as she turned back to look at Isla.

'Mindy's dead too.'

Isla started to cry even more, though she didn't make a sound as the tears began to flood her eyes.

'Why are Mum and Mindy dead?' Isla asked.

'Oh, Isla. Just… just know that it wasn't your fault and that they loved you very much... are you thirsty? I bet you are. Can I get you a drink? Or what about a blanket? You look cold. I think I have one in the car. I'll go and have a look. I'll be back in a minute.'

Mona smiled and then turned and left the office while Isla cried. As soon as the door shut behind her, Mona silently fell to her knees in a river of tears, realising that she knew exactly how Isla was feeling. Mona had lost a parent, and she had taken someone's mother away from them forever. She felt guilty and hateful. Shameful. Mona knew that Isla didn't deserve that. No one deserved that. Isla was too innocent, sweet and pure. She was just a little girl.

Mona's motives changed. She vowed that no matter what, she would keep Isla safe and away from harm, regardless of the plan."

Chapter Thirteen

"The night had gone, and the city's early morning go-getters flaunted their vitality at the sulks of those who lived their lives in a quiet desperation to escape the unfortunate hand they had to play with. It was a picturesque time of day, though the early red sky posed a threat to more than just those who sailed the water—for many, another Saturday morning had been gifted with being Mancunian.

I followed Rex in Conor O'Brien's black Range Rover to the yard where Isla was being held. He drove ahead in his white transit van. We were both armed with SA80 rifles and were wearing bandoliers that were carrying one hundred and fifty rounds, not to mention the thirty rounds that we had already cocked and made ready in our weapons. Only God could have helped us if we were to get pulled over by the law.

Michael had told us that a car with four men had recently arrived at the O'Brien's yard. They were all heavily armed and were men he recognised from around the city. As far as we knew, the odds were nine on three, though I was unsure how competent Mona would be in a gunfight.

We linked up with Michael just down the road from the O'Brien's yard. I'd never met him before. He was a tall, skinny black man with long dreadlocks and looked to be around the same age as me. Michael also looked like he'd experienced more life than the average man in their mid-thirties. A big scar ran down the side of his neck. There was a look about him, a seriousness in his eyes. I could tell he'd seen more than enough not to be easily shaken, especially working for Rex over the previous decade.

He was wearing a matching grey Nike tracksuit, zipped up halfway with no T-shirt underneath so that you could see his golden chain and the start of his six-pack. On his feet were a pair of expensive red Nike trainers.

Rex told Michael the plan. He then handed him a rifle and a bandolier of one hundred and fifty rounds. Michael was very calm when receiving the weapon and handled it in a way that suggested the normality of his world was a cry from civility. He loaded, cocked and made his rifle ready with ease. He felt like a man who could be trusted; I was confident he would deliver and help us get Isla back.

Rex and I had done our best to collimate the rifle scopes back at his house, but the aim wouldn't be one hundred per cent without zeroing the rifles properly. At that hour, and in the space we had available, it was the best we could do. I wasn't sure about them, but it would only ever take me a shot or two to learn how to adjust my aim to hit the sweet spot.

'Just remember, I'm up, I'm running, he sees me, I'm down. Stick to that, and they won't hit you, or will at least find it hard to. Manoeuvre yourself out of the line of fire. If you're a sitting duck, they'll drop you. Try and preserve your ammunition, too. Once we're out, we're out, and we don't know how much they have. Nevertheless, you need to be firing an aimed shot at least every six seconds to keep them under pressure.' I told the two gangsters confidently. It felt like being back in the army again. It was a feeling that I hadn't known in years. Almost a thrill that I didn't think I would ever feel again. I just wished it was under different circumstances.

'I like it. Murder, mayhem, mutilation. Maximum fucking violence.' Rex announced with a chuckle of laughter. His tight white T-shirt made his muscles look even more intimidating.

'Yes, G!' Michael said calmly while slowly nodding.

I gave Michael the key to the yard's back gate. He fist-bumped us both, and we climbed back into our motors to park them in front of a neighbouring warehouse, out of sight from the O'Briens. Then Michael walked his rifle around the back, using the same route Mo and I had used all those years ago.

Rex and I stayed in the driving seats of our vehicles. Luckily, no one would come in or out of the road to witness what was about to happen. Rex had assured me that there wouldn't be anyone about until Monday morning when the workers would start for the week.

The time was just before six o'clock. The air was still. Michael had until ten past the hour to get to the back gate. He would find it a lot easier than Mo and I had found it.

The sight of the passage gave me chills. I physically shivered upon seeing it lit up in the sober light of the morning; it was so surreal. I found it hard not to dwell on the memory.

There was no sign of movement at the yard, just the sound of the passing trains going in and out of the city. Michael said that he had seen them all go inside the office. They must have still been in there. I couldn't hear any of them from my position further down the road, even with the car windows ajar.

Knowing that Isla was there, just a few hundred meters away, was traumatising beyond compare. I desperately watched the minutes on the clock slowly change, tense with anticipation and eager to make a move. My sweaty head was wired. My denim jeans and black T-shirt were mostly dry, though I could still smell the river. Something about that smell, the smell of the ground and the murky water, always fuelled something within me. Something almost electric that was born in the back fields of Catterick. It heightened my senses and gave me a mental edge. I was ready.

The clock turned to ten past six. Rex drove off, passed the front gate and went to the opposite side of the yard. He then parked up at the side of the road and started playing

ACDC music at full volume. The opening guitar riff cried out across the yard, making the pigeons flee from the scene.

Three big and tough-looking men came out of the office. They were loaded with rifles and keen to learn where the music was coming from. Rex started firing, and the men ducked down beneath the covers of the cars parked in the yard.

That was my cue. I drove along the road at speed and turned to enter the open front gate of the yard, using Rex's gunfire as cover. Once I was in, I drifted ninety degrees to the right so that the passenger door faced the office and got out of the driver's side.

I used the bonnet of Connor O'Brien's Range Rover for cover, flicked off my safety and leant over the front of the car to fire two aimed shots at the men in front of the office. The smell of the gunfire caressed my senses. I'd missed that lethal scent. It ignited the marksman within me. The rounds being fired blasted through my ears like heavenly drums. I ducked down behind the car and gripped the rifle like a long-lost lover before rising again above the cover of safety to fire at the enemy. Just like that, I was back in war mode.

ACDC continued to play loudly. Rounds were being fired back at us. We were in a gunfight.

To begin with, we weren't having much luck. The O'Brien's men were digging in with their eyeballs, frozen with fear and staying tight to the ground.

Rex managed to get one of them out of their hiding spot. I caught sight and finished him off with a shot to the head before ducking down again to take cover. The back of his head exploded as he fell to the ground. One down, eight to go.

I jumped and dived to use another car for cover. Shots were being fired at me. Then, more shots came from that direction, but they started sounding like they were coming from further away. That was Michael. He had entered the fight and was firing from the back of the yard. Rex and I fired with him every two to six seconds to optimise the pressure.

Rex, still outside the yard by his van, started making his way up the side road that led around the back of the yard. He was using the cars parked within as cover. I saw him up and running for a few seconds before diving to the ground to retake cover. His agility amazed me for someone who was nearly fifty.

I continued to fire until I got a stoppage. I took a knee and ejected my magazine before reloading another.

Then I was back in and firing. Shots were embedding themselves into cars from all directions.

By that point, the fourth man and Johnny Allen had joined the other two outside to help defend the office. Rounds were flying over my head and hitting whatever was in their path. I could hear glass shattering behind me as the rounds hit the windows.

In the distance, I saw Michael rise and fire a shot that managed to get a man in the neck. The man grabbed his throat as blood rushed out of it. He then dropped to the ground, hitting his head hard on the boot of a car as he fell. Two down, seven to go.

I looked over the bonnet, fired two shots and then ran and dived behind another car three meters away to get a different angle on the enemy's position. Shots of fire were still coming from all over. Rounds were going past my head as I landed on the concrete. A round buried itself into a car behind me while another smashed the window of the vehicle I was shielding behind, spraying shattered glass all over my back. I brushed it off as best as I could, but I didn't have time to worry about minor cuts. Instead, I reacted with three rounds, narrowly missing one of their men as he quickly dug into the ground.

I caught sight of Rex. He looked to be in his element, smiling and laughing as he rose above the cars outside the fence to take shots at the city's rival gang. He had been waiting for a reason to have a proper pop at the O'Briens for years.

Our plan was working. We had them covered from three angles. I was firing from the front, Michael from the back, and Rex from the side. Michael and I made sure to stay out of each other's line of fire. The last thing we wanted was for one of us to meet our demise, let alone from a friendly round.

Liam O'Brien and Hector joined Allen and the other men outside. Mona and Paddy Wang stayed inside the office. It was five on three outside in the fight.

I heard a scream. Rex had hit another one in the leg. That directed most of their gunfire his way. I aimed over the top of the car and caught the injured man in the arm twice before crouching back down. I looked underneath the car and could see him lying on the ground. His rifle was away from his grip. Then I saw the top of his head explode.

'Yes, you fuck!' I heard Rex shout. Three down, six to go.

The firing continued as each man ducked and manoeuvred to secure a better defensive position. The fight had taken a turn, and every man left firing had learned from the fallen how to defend and attack efficiently to advance their competence. It was a proper gunfight.

I jumped behind another car to my right and then moved forward to another vehicle to get a better look. I had a great view of everything that was going on, apart from Rex's position. I could see Michael. Gallant and critical. He rose over the top of a car, took an aimed shot, and nearly caught a man. Then he was back down again. Michael rose and fired. He caught a man on the shoulder. The round burst through the man's back. I jumped up and fired two shots at his head. The man fell and hit the ground. Four down, five to go.

Before Michael could get behind the cover of safety, Allen rose and pulled his trigger. He injured Michael on the right shoulder. Michael's shoulder flung backwards, and he lost control of his rifle. The weapon hit the ground while Michael stood there, too shocked by the pain to drop. In the split of a second, Allen rose again and fired. The round went through the air and hit Michael in the head. I saw him look up to the sky as he slowly hit the ground. Shit. Michael was down and out of the fight. We'd lost him...

It was three on two, but they had an extra two in reserve with Mona and Paddy Wang inside the office.

The sound of a different ACDC song played in the background. I had to concentrate, or it would have been me that was dead next. I couldn't let that happen. I wouldn't let that happen.

One of the O'Brien's men shot the tyre of a car I was using for cover. The tyre sounded like a grenade exploding.

I jumped up and aimed but couldn't see any enemy position. To keep the threat of attack imminent, I shot at a likely place where they could be taking cover and then hit the ground again behind a car. Seconds later, I heard Rex do the same.

I looked below the undercarriage and saw a pair of feet in the distance. I quickly got into the prone position, breathed in, exhaled and fired at their ankles. A deep, bellowing scream called out. I took another shot at the same ankle and hit my target. The scream cried louder as I shattered the man's ankle to pieces. The one-footed man was swearing and yelling profusely in agony as he fell. Then I heard an enemy shot being fired in Rex's direction. I panicked.

'Fucking missed!' shouted Rex. I sighed in relief and rose slightly above the car.

Then, out of the corner of my eye, I saw the door to the office open. It was Paddy Wang, and he was holding a rifle.

Paddy Wang had flipped his rifle to automatic. He fired rounds like a machine gun from his right to left. Spraying over half the yard with gunfire as he did so. The sound was colossal. Glass shattered through the air as car windows from all around smashed to pieces. I didn't know where Rex was, but I hoped he was digging in with his eyelids like I was and didn't come up for air any time soon.

The rifle ran out of ammunition, and Paddy Wang retreated into the office to take cover.

I stayed down for a moment, looking for movement beneath the cars and waiting to see who would fire next.

'Yes, you fat fuck!' Rex shouted from his side of the yard. Then I heard Rex fire twice. It was Liam O'Brien whose ankle had been shattered. He was suffering badly down on the ground, and Rex had just shot him in the chest and then the face. The second O'Brien brother was dead. There was just Allen, Hector, Paddy Wang, and Mona remaining.

The firing continued in my direction as the trains continued to go in and out of the city. I heard a brief pause and moved quickly to a different car.

Then I saw him through the car windows—Hector. He was about thirty meters away from me but facing the other way. I crouched down low into the prone position, made my rifle safe, and crawled forward across the tarmac to get closer. I wanted a headshot without a car in the way.

I lifted my rifle and aimed at his head. He was there for the taking. I clicked the safety off and hovered my finger over the trigger. I was just about to squeeze to send Hector to meet his maker before suddenly, his head burst at the sound of someone else's gunfire.

'Yes, you wanker!' I heard Rex shout while laughing. He had beaten me to the shot.

I got to my feet, still hunched below the car's roof, and moved around to get closer to the office. Rex covered me with gunfire. I ran and jumped down on the ground, then rose above the boot of a car, searching for an enemy position. I was happy with the distance I had covered; not much further, and I would have been at the office. I planned to burst in and shoot Paddy Wang in the head and save Isla. I was confident that Rex would take care of Johnny Allen, and that Mona would be too frozen with fear to fire her pistol at me.

Then I saw movement at the office door. I looked up in horror. My heart was in my throat.

Mona was there. She was holding Isla in front of her while Paddy Wang aimed a rifle at my little girl's head. Isla looked horrified as she stood there barefoot and crying. She could see me.

'Isla! Don't worry, I'm coming!' I shouted to her.

'Allen!' Paddy Wang screamed. His rifle was still aimed at her head. I didn't know whether to fire at him. It was too risky; I could have hit Isla, or Paddy Wang might have shot her by accident.

A car engine started. The three of them hurried to a Range Rover parked just meters away from the office door. Mona opened the back and pulled Isla in with her. Paddy Wang shut the door and ran around the front to the passenger side.

I heard a shot go off. Rex had caught Paddy Wang on the shoulder. He screamed in pain and held his bleeding arm while climbing into the front of the car. The door shut behind him, and the car drove off.

I panicked. I couldn't see the wheels to aim at through all the parked cars in front of me. Isla looked so scared. I needed to get to her.

I chased after the car, but it was too quick for me. I jumped over car bonnets and sprinted as fast as I could run, but by the time I had gotten near it, they had turned out of the gates and were speeding down the road away from the yard.

An instant later, Rex pulled up in his van. I quickly ran around the front and opened the passenger door. While I had one foot in the van, he drove off to catch up with them.

I pulled myself in and closed the door behind me. Rex turned down the music, and we chased them through the city.

That was the second time in six hours that Rex and I had driven away from a bloodshed mess."

Chapter Fourteen

"I can't help but think about one particular morning. 2019, I think it was.

I was ripped softly from my dream to awake in a reality more breathtaking than any other world could comprehend. Mindy's gentle lips kissed my cheek again and again until I woke. The hot morning sun, the sound of the birds chirping away at each other, and the soft naked arms of my wife angelically begging for attention as she nibbled tenderly on my ear surpassed any realm of desire. The only disturbance that would enhance the moment further came when Isla ran into our bedroom and jumped on top of the covers to be quickly embraced by Mindy's loving arms.

'Mum won't wake up.' my daughter told us.

'Maybe she's tired, sweety.' Mindy explained while running her hand through Isla's hair.

'She's snoring on the sofa, and she's spilt a bottle of wine all over the floor.' said Isla.

'Well, at least she's breathing.' I said sarcastically, mourning the four-month life of the new living room carpet.

'Yesterday Mum said she'd make me pancakes for breakfast.'

'Okay. I'll come and wake your mum up, and then we'll make pancakes together. How's that sound?' said Mindy.

'Can I have blueberries and syrup? Actually, can I have one with blueberries and one with chocolate buttons?'

'Yes, Chef. Go and try to wake your mum up. I'll be down in thirty seconds.' Mindy said, laughing a little.

Isla's smile beamed from ear to ear as she got up and dived on me to give me the biggest hug ever.

'Morning, Dad.'

'Good morning. Did you sleep well?' I replied while hugging my daughter tightly.

'Yeah.' Isla said happily before getting up and jumping off the bed to run to the kitchen.

Mindy turned and kissed me on the lips as our bodies intertwined.

'I love you.' she whispered in my ear before kissing me on the cheek and getting out of the bed.

She looked back and smiled at me as she walked nakedly towards the back of the bedroom door to get her dressing gown, laughing quietly to herself as she caught me looking at her perfect bum.

'Come on. Pancakes.' she said as she tied a bow on the front of her white robe.

'I'll be down in a minute.' I replied. Mindy smiled and left the bedroom."

Chapter Fifteen

"After they fled the yard, Rex and I aggressively chased them out of the city. Allen was an exceptional driver, and his skills were being demonstrated on the road. He managed to evade us at every attempt to overtake them.

I was drenched in desperation. We were so close. The aching of the chase tore at my insides. I'd never wanted anything more than to stop that car and get my little girl away from it all. In my mind, I kept playing out different scenarios of how she would be feeling or how they were treating her.

The type of death owed to her kidnappers depended on her condition once I had gotten her back. If Isla were unharmed, then it would be a quick death for all; although I didn't think that I'd be able to shoot Mona, I knew I'd have to leave her for Rex. However, If they had hurt Isla in any way, then I would slowly devour their prayers, inflicting insidious pain as their bodies bled to ruin. What would your father do?"

"My father? We have a… complicated relationship.

Jack, Mona was lovingly hugging Isla in the back of the Range Rover. Keeping her safe and shielding her from the madness of the world they passed through. If it weren't for Mona, Paddy Wang would have put a round in the back of Isla's head during the shoot-out at the yard.

Mona instantly felt a maternally unconditional love for Isla the moment they first locked eyes. She had never experienced a feeling like that before, such a desire to keep another from harm. It weakened her and made her re-

evaluate both the days passed and the future awaiting. She loved her.

Paddy Wang was sat in the passenger seat, clutching onto his gun-wounded arm, squirming from the pain. Sweat dripped down his forehead as his fever grew. His white shirt was drenched with a mix of blood and sweat.

'You need to tie something around it. Your arm. Stop the bleeding.' said Allen, never taking his eyes off the road. He was finding Paddy Wang's groans distracting.

'I fucking know! Where are the fucking cigarettes? And where the fuck are we going!?' Paddy Wang replied angrily.

'I'm trying to lose them. I thought leaving the city would be our best bet before the streets are too full to move. It's only a matter of time til the boys in blue come crawling. Here, take these.' Allen passed Paddy Wang a pack of cigarettes and a lighter from his jacket pocket.

'Well, what a shit fucking job you're doing; they're all I've seen in the mirror for the past twenty-five minutes.' Paddy Wang lit a cigarette and lowered his window ajar. The rushing noise of the air attacking the car's interior through the lowered glass frightened Isla. Isla's tears were dampening Mona's top. She silently cried while cuddled up on Mona's lap with her head buried into her chest. The only comfort she could find was in Mona's sweet scent. That same smell that aroused your affection for her all those years ago.

Mona had lost her nerve but was trying hard not to show it. The night had not panned out as planned. Nine people had died, and the victim of it all had somehow become the aggressor. Two of her cousins were dead, and that terrified her. Mona didn't know what you were capable of before that morning. She thought you were the same boy she knew all those years ago, and in many ways, you were, but in even more ways, you had grown. You had evolved to become a ferocious flame in the fury of firearms.

Disciplined and effective. Relentless and resilient. You are a killer, Jack, trained by some of the finest soldiers the world has ever known. Mona knew that there would be a price to pay for the murder of Mindy and an even bigger price if Isla was harmed.

The Range Rover sped down the bumpy back country roads of the northwest. The city's architecture had long been replaced by hilly fields, farmland, and the English countryside, absent from traffic and free of pedestrians—as you know.

Mona's head had gone. All the overthinking had changed her motives yet again. She had decided that if she was to die, you all were, too, and found a romantic solace in the tragedy as if it was some sort of poetic justice to season the mess.

Her newly found shame had suddenly vanished. All retribution had perished over the last couple of hours as her illicit mind became free from corruption. Isla's eyes were almost like the antidote to the poison of her vengeance.

However, as the morning sun shone, Mona's vampiric vendetta had grown again, like an infection immunising itself from a course of antibiotics. The anguish had swallowed her in a devilish despair.

Mona closed her eyes and tightened her grip on Isla, clenching as if the harder she squeezed, the more her cravings were satisfied. She became delirious, floating and sinking all at once as the child's head pressed harder and harder into her chest. She intended to kill Isla and then fire her pistol at both you and Rex in the head before killing the two men sitting in front of her. Then, finally, she would shoot herself and join her dad and the rest of you in the afterlife.

Her heart pounded faster and faster as she fantasised an imagery of the little girl's skull bursting in her arms and seeing the look of broken defeat in your sorry eyes before

*killing you. Her squeeze continued to tighten as her thirst
for revenge was quenched. A tragedy that felt righteous in
her backwardly ill mind.*

*‘Mona.’ said Isla through the tears in a mouse-like,
frightened voice. Mona’s grip loosened, and she softly
pulled back Isla’s head to look into the little girl’s eyes.
Mona gasped as she saw them—the same eyes as yours.
The little girl's face cuddled her heart with love, instantly
warming the ice in her sinister veins. Mona’s confusion
derailed her homicidal motives, and mercy prevailed in a
maternal glow. It bloomed out of the ashes of her psychotic
darkness.*

*Her plan had changed. Mona still intended to kill you
all. But she would allow both herself and Isla to survive.
She would then raise your daughter as her own, and they
would live happily ever after on the money you had made.*

*Isla silently cried while Mona gently pulled the girl to
her chest. She kissed the top of Isla’s head while stroking
her hair.*

*‘Don’t worry, Isla. Everything’s fine.’ said Mona
angelically.*

*‘No, no, it’s not fucking fine!’ shouted Paddy Wang from
the front, who had just taken his shirt off to assess the
damage to his arm. The round from the rifle hadn’t gone
completely through. Instead, it had slashed across his
deltoid muscle and had taken a chunk of the flesh with it.*

*‘Will you live?’ Allen asked as he came back onto the left
side of the road after overtaking a tractor.*

‘Shut the fuck up!’ Paddy Wang replied angrily.”

“That bitch… She was always mental; the whole time we
were together, she was always a little… dark and twisted…
like a killer clown chewing on a popped balloon.

How is it that you know so much, anyway?” asked Jack.

"All in good time, my friend." the cigar-smoking man replied with a smile that could charm the darkest of souls. He then took a sip of his whisky and hinted to Jack to continue with the story.

"Okay.

In the van behind, Rex had done well to keep up with them.

'Where the fuck are these perverts going!? See if you can get the back wheels down.' Rex thought aloud.

'No, might make them crash. Isla could get hurt.' I replied.

'Something's got to give. We can't keep on like this all fucking morning.' said Rex. He was right. Every time we got closer, Allen managed to widen the gap. Many a time, we nearly lost them as they sped away after taking a turn. But Rex was too good. He'd had a passion for speed since his teen years.

Helplessly watching the chase ahead of me was becoming too much to handle. I needed to do something. I couldn't sit back as a spectator to disaster anymore.

'Fuck it. You're right. I'm gonna put a bit of pressure on them.' I told Rex after a few minutes of silently debating the options, with a growing concern for the ever-lowering level of petrol in the van. I needed to coarse them into a newer panic and change their tactics to give us an opening of attack.

'Drive steady.' I told Rex.

'I've got you.'

I undid my seatbelt and picked up my rifle. After checking over the weapon, I lowered my window and pushed the safety button off. The wind roared as we drove—it was deafening. Rex lowered his window slightly to stabilise the vehicle and help with the noise.

I hung out the side of the van, trying to leave every part of me below my ribcage inside so that I didn't fall out. With my rifle, I aimed at the passenger side. The bumps of the road were making it impossible to find a good shot. I was hesitant to fire. Even though the sight picture was only bouncing around slightly, I knew that it would have a big impact on where my round ended up. I didn't want to accidentally shoot Isla, and I was concerned that I would make the Range Rover crash.

The country road was long and straight for some time. There were acres of open, flat, grassy fields on both sides. On the right, the grass stretched out for miles. On the left was a large woodland a few hundred meters away from the road.

I concentrated on my breathing, focusing on the shot in hand as the two vehicles sped along. Being in the passenger seat made it an awkward shot. It meant that I had to hang out of the window even more than I had wanted just to be able to aim properly with the butt of the rifle cemented firmly into my right shoulder. Rex understood and hung onto my ankle to stop me from falling out.

I dangled out the side of the van. The wind pelted me in the face aggressively, drowning me in oxygen. I tightened my grip and drove the weapon back into my body for support. The reticle of my rifle scope was still quivering, but less so once my grip was secured. I exhaled all my breath out of my lungs, concentrated and pulled the trigger.

The sound of gunfire blasted through my ears. The passenger side wing mirror of the Range Rover exploded into pieces. It was a lucky shot. I had been aiming at the passenger window rather than the mirror.

Again, I looked through the LDS scope, but I was still struggling to fix a point.

'Take the wheel. She'll be alright!' Rex shouted through the noise.

I nudged my rifle down slightly to aim at the passenger-side wheel and fired a second shot. The round burst through the spokes, and the rubber tread of the wheel popped. There was a booming sound as the wheel exploded. Sparks flew out like fireworks as Allen lost control of the speeding vehicle thirty meters or so ahead of us.

Rex anticipated a crash. He quickly pulled me back in while breaking as softly as he could to avoid both colliding into the back of the car and me being smashed through the windshield."

"You're right, Jack. Allen couldn't control it. He tried to balance the vehicle, but he made things worse. The car drove off the road onto the flat grassy field to the left. He had taken his foot off the accelerator, but they were still moving at speed. Allen was hopelessly holding onto the uncontrollable steering wheel as it span with force from left to right and back again. Paddy Wang swung his good arm around and held onto the back of his headrest. Mona was the only one with a seat belt on. She held onto Isla tightly as the car drove through the open field until it eventually came to a halt halfway between the road and the woodland."

"Rex had pulled over, and we were both already out of the van with our rifles in our hands. They, too, then got out of the car and were running. Allen and Paddy Wang both had rifles, and Mona had Isla in her arms and flung over her right shoulder as the three of them ran towards the cover of the woods ahead of them. I needed to get to her.

I took a knee and aimed my rifle in their direction. They were only around seventy meters away. I would hit them with ease, firing from stable ground. I couldn't afford to hit Isla by accident, so I aimed for the runner's legs.

At the back was Paddy Wang. I watched his little legs try to catch up with the others as he fell behind. Half of his shirt was soaked with blood.

I concentrated and fired a shot at his left ankle. He screamed as the round entered his bone, and he fell to the ground before getting back up and hobbling on slowly. I felt a slight admiration for the fight he had in him to try and continue to run, though he was barely covering any ground.

'Bit of a leg man, are ya? Fucking pervert.' Rex said jokingly.

Rex and I ran towards the hobbling man. We caught up with him in no time. Rex hit the butt of his rifle over the back of the little man's head, and he fell face-first to the ground after making an emasculated grunt.

'You go, I'll deal with this one.' said Rex. I nodded and ran after the others, who had just entered the woods."

"Rex. He's never failed to amuse me. He's a dear friend of mine, as he is yours, Jack.

'Well, Paddy the pervert. What say you? How you feeling, mate?' said Rex as he pointed the barrel of his rifle in Paddy Wang's face. The O'Brien brother had rolled over and was lying with his back to the ground.

'Fuck you, Rex.' replied Paddy Wang.

'Fuck me? No… no, not fuck me. Fuck you… I sentence thee to death, mate. You, ya fucking little… na, come on, look at me. Look me in the eye. Look me in the eye, you slag. You look like shit, mate. Proper… Yeah. You… well, you are well and truly fucked, mate. The sins you have committed on this Godfearing world are indefensible. Fucking condemnable. When you meet your maker, and you will, he's gonna slide you on your way down to hell like the fucking snake you are, mate, where I'm sure a little thing like you is likely to be fucked in the face, every day, by some big geezer who's got a bit of a temper. What say you?' said Rex.

'My men know about all this. They will come for you. They will burn everything you have, everyone you love, everything you've built. The streets will be fucking carnage. Really, it's you who's fucked, mate.' Paddy Wang said boldly before spitting in the direction of Rex's boots. A bit of his spit landed on the end of the big man's toecaps.

'Well, see, that was uncalled for. Not fucking nice. What have my boots ever done to you? Ay? Used to spitting, though aint ya I've heard. Gotta give it a good spit before you drive It home… Those poor boys.'

'Fuck off!'

'Paddy Wang… do you like Pina coladas?' Rex then shot the little man in the face. The third brother's dead eyes stared into the sun as blood flowed from a bullet wound at the centre of his forehead.

Rex fired a second and then a third round into his head to make sure he was dead. Rex looked at the dead man with no emotion and then flung the barrel of his rifle over his right shoulder so that the muzzle was facing the sky. He strolled casually towards the woods while singing quietly to himself.

'If you like making love at midnight.'"

Jack nearly smiled but then remembered what came next.

"I'd been chasing them for over five minutes through the branches and the tree trunks. I hadn't been able to see the world outside for a while. I was sweating profusely, but not just because I was moving at speed; the anxiety of not being able to get to my little girl was spiralling my mind into a plague panic. I was fearful for the first time that I might not be able to save her and that after hearing the gunshots that killed Paddy Wang, they understood they were headed to meet him in the afterlife a lot sooner than they had planned. I feared they had decided to kill Isla already.

I couldn't find them. Everywhere looked the same. The deciduous trees covered the sky. Very few rays of light shone through the gaps between the bloomed leaves. The rugged ground was covered with twigs and roots. The silence was clear. My breathing was the loudest thing around. I needed to get that under control.

The uneven terrain made it difficult to run. I was concerned about breaking a twig beneath my boots; the noise would have compromised my position. I was used to being in that environment, but those longing thoughts of desperation were unprecedented. I wanted to call out for Isla, but I knew that would just make me the easiest of targets. My breathing got worse as my panic grew. I couldn't help it. I needed to see she was okay.

Using the trees as cover, I moved from trunk to trunk through the woodland with heightened senses, listening and looking for any signs of activity. There was no movement, not even from any wildlife.

Then, randomly, I was hesitant to advance. Something felt off, and I could sense that I was being watched. I crouched slightly and slowly scanned my arcs. I knew they were close.

The sound of gunfire provoked my attention as the bark flew off a tree next to me. If Allen were a better shot, he would have killed me.

I hit the ground quickly and observed the direction that the round came from. My leg landed on a large log. It hurt, but I would be over the pain soon enough.

They were nowhere to be seen. I waited while slowly guiding my scope from left to right for any signs of movement. Still, I couldn't locate them. The smell of the ground had worked its way into my nostrils. My military training was instinctive. I knew what to look for. I had been trained to find hidden killers in the shadows of war. I looked for their human shape and any signs of shadows or silhouettes. I looked for any shine bouncing from their accessories and the possible spacing between them. Nature doesn't rest as we do; there are no straight lines in nature. I was also looking out for any sudden movement among the trees.

Still, after minutes, I couldn't see them. I knew they couldn't be far away, as I was obviously within shooting range. I also knew they hadn't left their hiding position.

I decided to run to a tree three meters to my right to see if I could get a better look from a different angle at where they were. Also, I could potentially draw out their position by encouraging Allen to take another shot if he saw me up and running. It was risky, but I had good faith that I would be back on the ground behind the cover of safety before he had the chance to hit me.

I took a deep breath, then got up and sprinted to the chosen tree, hitting the greenery and hardened mud on the ground as I landed.

My plan worked. Just as I hit the ground, he fired again. I was too quick for him. The sound of his shot gave me a better indication of their position.

Back in the prone, I scanned the area through my scope from where the shot came. For a moment, I couldn't see anything. It was incredibly frustrating. Time passed by while my heart tried to beat itself out of my chest.

But then I saw something. Something pink, sticking out the side of a tree. It must have been Isla's Pyjamas, around fifty meters away.

My breathing slowed as I examined her position, looking for signs of Mona or Allen. I moved my view left to the neighbouring tree. At first, I didn't see anything, just the wilderness. But then I saw the barrel of Allen's rifle slowly moving as he looked for me. I made out his shoulder and head behind overgrown grass and leaves. He was well hidden. I hated to admit it, but I was impressed with his efforts of concealment. He had ripped out some grass and mud and chucked it on his back and head to blend in more with his surroundings.

I was low on the ground, feeling confident I, too, was well hidden. My scope fixed onto his skull. I was going for the kill shot. My breathing slowed even more as I relaxed, making sure my position and hold of the weapon was firm. I took a deep breath in and then exhaled. I didn't inhale again. I left my lungs without oxygen as the reticle of my scope covered Allen's face. Still on an out breath, I put my finger to the trigger.

Gunfire echoed around the trees, and mud jumped up from next to my head. Just as I was about to squeeze to send Allen to meet his maker, he had fired, and he had struck the ground next to me and then rolled around to the cover of a tree.

I was angry; it was one of the few times he had ever beaten me to anything first.

Looking ahead, without the use of my scope, I saw Allen and Mona run further away into the woods. Isla was over Mona's shoulder. One of Mona's hands was shielding Isla's head from harm as they dodged under and around pointy branches and tree trunks to flee for their lives.

My rifle was aimed at Allen, and I pulled the trigger at his efforts to escape. He managed to avoid the hit with a slight zigzag of a run, ducking and dodging like a rugby player.

I got to my feet and ran after them. The uneven terrain made it hard to move. I could see them, but I struggled to catch up.

Ducking under branches, swerving around trees and trying not to trip over was something I considered a game back when I was in the military. However, I was too desperate to get Isla back to find the fun in it.

I could see her—Isla. My heart melted at how close she was. It was like a chemical fix that had entered my bloodstream or the deflation of an inflammation of emotion. I had to push harder and catch up with them. No pain would ever compare to what it would feel for me to have let her slip away after getting that close. I was sprinting as fast as I could. My lungs were in rag, but breathing could wait. I would breathe again when Isla was safe and in my arms.

Ahead, Mona started to slow down. The weight of carrying Isla had burned up her energy. I guess she was tired and hungry and found it hard to get around the obstacles in the woodland. It would have been hard enough even without the extra weight of carrying a seven-year-old girl.

Mona wasn't looking properly where she was running and tripped on a root. She fell with Isla still in her arms. The pair of them hit the ground hard. Mona hit a tree as she fell and cut her forehead.

Allen turned around and, in a panic, fired at me again. I managed to anticipate his shot and got behind the cover of a trunk around thirty meters away from them just before he pulled the trigger.

Allen was behind a tree next to where the girls lay. Mona was up. A small amount of blood was pouring out of the cut on her forehead. Isla wasn't hurt much, but still, it was a nasty fall. Luckily, she had landed mainly on the mud and the grass and was sitting up and looking at Mona. Mona turned to Isla and cradled my daughter in her arms on the floor.

'Isla!' I shouted.

'Dad!?... Dad!' I heard her little voice shout back. She sounded excited and hopeful to hear me. But I could tell she was scared. It was so good to hear her voice.

'Dad!' she shouted again.

'It's okay, I'm coming.'

'You're too late, Duke. I'm gonna shoot her, and then I'm gonna shoot you!' Allen shouted.

'You better get her back to me!' I called out.

'You're not the one running this, alright? I am. It's over, Duke. You're gonna tell me where you keep your stash of money, or I'm going to shoot her in the fucking head!' shouted Allen.

'Get fucked, you hat!' I replied.

'Tell me now, or I'll shoot them both!' he shouted desperately.

'You can shoot Mona, save me a fucking job!'

'Where's the money!? Mona, get out the way of the girl!' shouted Allen.

'No!' Mona screamed while she sat on the ground, shielding Isla from Allen. Tears and blood poured down her face as she cradled Isla in her arms.

'Mona! Get out the fucking way!' Allen shouted. He was only a few meters away from them, but he was too scared to move away from the tree; he knew I would shoot him.

My heart seized up. I didn't know what was going to happen. My rifle grip got tighter as I prepared to move around the tree trunk to fire at speed. Undoubtedly, I could kill Allen from that distance with ease. It was like second nature to me. I had spent years practising my marksmanship skills, both out on the range and in the theatre of war. I could confidently take both Allen and Mona out in seconds. However, the cost was too great. I needed to get Isla to safety first.

'Mona!?' Allen shouted again. Still, there was no reply from the shielding woman. She just continued to cry while Isla's head was buried into her chest.

I could see Allen. His rifle was aimed in my direction, but he kept changing his head position away from me to look at Mona. It was sinking in for him that Mona was no longer playing along with the plan. It was just them two left. Everyone else was dead, and they both knew that.

Allen was visibly distressed, angry, and bitter. He had the eyes of a madman, but most of all, he was scared; I could hear it in his voice.

I, too, was terrified. Terrified of his next move. He had nothing left to lose. If he was to fire at Mona, the round would likely go straight through her and into Isla, killing them both. I couldn't let that happen. I needed to act fast.

'Allen, you can stop this, you can stop all of it! Give me Isla, and I'll tell you where the money is.' I shouted.

'Dad!' Isla shouted again.

'Don't worry, Isla!' I shouted back.

'Fuck off, Duke, you've had this coming for a long time! You ruined my fucking life! Tell me where it is now!' said Allen.

'You're fucking mental! We've been over this. If you weren't such a fucking arsehole, you would have passed P company. You need to take responsibility for yourself, mate. It's really not my problem. Mona, get Isla to me now!' I shouted.

'Fuck off! I should have been a para! I should have been 1 Para! It was your mates that got me kicked off SF selection, too. Tell me where the money is!' Allen shouted.

His head moved back to face Mona and Isla. Then that voice came again. That inner voice. The one inside my head. The one I always listened to. The one that was the inducement for both my successes and failures. The voice I had been ignoring for Isla's sake. That little inveigle voice that just said

'Fuck it.'

In a split second, I aimed my rifle and fired at Allen. I caught him in the chest, just below the neck. Both of our bodies jolted backwards as we hit the ground simultaneously. He had a tortured and arrogant smile upon his lips as he fell, suggesting he had still somehow won. As he dropped and hit the ground, his rifle fell away from his hold, and his body lay there, bleeding into the land.

I felt it straight away, but I tried to hide it. It hurt. It hurt a lot. I was struggling to breathe. It was as if I was choking on nothing, but I held it back. I had to mask my suffering. Isla still wasn't safe and in my arms.

I got to my feet and looked at the girls. Mona was pointing her pistol at me. At the same time that I had fired at Allen, she had hit me in the ribs with the weapon that had killed both my wife and Isla's mother.

Mona then tried to fire a second shot at me but got a stoppage. She had run out of rounds.

Isla, still barefoot, ran to me as Mona sat on the ground in a state of frozen terror while I aimed my rifle at her head.

Isla hugged my leg as tight as she could. It felt so good to know that my daughter was safe again.

Mona looked at me with a delirious, witchlike glare.

'What you gonna do, Jackson Duke? Shoot me? You won't shoot me.' said Mona in an arrogant tone, suggesting my aim was a bluff.

'You killed my wife. You killed Cara. You took my little girl.'

My torso was in excruciating pain. I could feel the blood pouring out, trickling down my skin like warm water.

Isla clutched harder onto my leg and shifted her head to look at Mona with daggers in her eyes. She was furious to learn that her new friend had killed both her mum and stepmum.

'You killed my dad, Jack!' Mona protested.

'I won't explain what happened again.' I replied.

'You fucking killed him! An eye for an eye, Jack. It's all over. You took one of mine, so I took two of yours. Now, it can be just us three… it can be just us. You, me and Isla. We could live so happily. We could put this all behind us. Just us against everyone. Just like it was, I know you still love me. I know you do.' she said while still sitting on the ground.

'Mona, we were together fourteen years ago. You're mental. I love Mindy, no one else. You've got to let it go, mate. You put Isla in danger. You're not going near her ever again.'

'Don't you fucking mate me! You love me!'

'No, Mona, I don't.'

'Yes, you do! You do! I know you do! We could be so happy together, just like we was. We could do all the things we talked about doing. It would be so perfect.' Mona was crying.

'No, Mona.'

'Yes!'

Tears were falling down her face.

'I know you love me, Jack.'

'I don't love you, Mona.'

'Yes! Yes, you do! Yes, you fucking do!' Mona then went to reach for Allen's rifle.

'I wouldn't fucking do that if I were you.' I told her. Isla buried her eyes into the side of my leg in a fright.

'You killed my fucking dad!' shouted Mona.

'Jesus… Fuck your dad, Mona! Fuck your dad, and fuck you! You've got five seconds to disappear before I shoot you in the fucking face, mate. Now go on. Fuck off!'

'Don't fucking mate me! I'm more than a mate! You know I hate it when you call me that!' she shouted through the tears.

'Five…four… three…' I counted down out loud.

Then I fell to the ground. The blood loss and the pain from the round in my body had weakened me so much that I could no longer stand. I collapsed. My head felt light, and my fingers lost their strength, though I still somehow managed to keep hold of my rifle as I fell.

Isla screamed.

'Dad!... Dad!' she shouted while kneeling over me with her hands on my cheek, panicking as she patted my face with love. I had lost too much blood. Isla knew that I was in trouble.

Mona crawled over and reached for Allen's rifle. She picked it up and got to her feet while aiming the weapon at my bleeding body. Isla looked up at her and gasped, frozen with fear as she stared down the barrel of the pointed rifle. I knew what was coming. I reached out for my daughter's hand and held it tightly. She was trembling. We were both scared. I couldn't save her. I had failed.

The sound of gunfire bounced off the tree trunks. Isla screamed. She was almost deafening in my ear. It was the same scream that I had heard that night when she had that awful nightmare. I had to go into her room to see if she was okay. I stayed with her that night and slept on her bedroom floor. When Mindy came in in the morning, we were both fast asleep. My arm was still raised onto her bed as I held her little hand all through the night.

Mona dropped to her knees. She was smiling. She had won. My first love fell to her side and lay there on the ground. The muscles in her smile relaxed as blood escaped through her heart-shaped mouth. She began to choke. It wasn't Mona who pulled the trigger. It wasn't me either.

Walking casually through the woods, he came. The man who had saved me time after time. It was Rex. He had found where we were and then shot Mona in the chest before she took her shot.

Rex then delivered a Coup de grâce in the form of a further two shots to Mona's head. To put her out of her misery. To free her from pain.

Isla's tears dripped onto my face as she knelt over me. Rex quickly came when he saw the state I was in and knelt on the other side.

'Hello, Little One. And you, ya pervert, need to have a word with yourself. You should have shot that lunatic woman right through the eyes.' said Rex.

'Rex. Daddy's hurt.' Isla said through her tears.

'It's alright, Little One. Your dad's gonna be fine. He has to be; he owes me a new bike.' Rex said jokingly while laughing a little.

'I'll get you a bike.' I replied through struggled breath.

'What, just like you got me a car? Funnily enough, there's a few cars going cheap down the O'Brien's place.' We both laughed. The laughter hurt, and I started to cough up blood.

'Ahh, don't make me laugh. Isla, I was so worried about you. I love you so much.' I said.

'I love you too, Daddy. Where's Mummy and Mindy?' Isla replied while crying.

'Darling, they… they were both… they're dead, sweety. I'm sorry. They were killed by the people who took you last night. But me and Rex got them. We got the people who killed them. They both loved you so, so much. So much. Just as I do, you're my best friend in the whole world. And…' I started to cough even more blood. Isla cried uncontrollably. Her tears fell on my face like rain.

'Daddy. Don't you die, Daddy. I love you too.'

'I'm not going anywhere. I will never leave you again. No matter where you go or what you do, I'll always be with you. Always.'

I held her hand and smiled, looking into her crying eyes. I always loved looking into her eyes. It was like looking into a younger and much prettier mirror. It's weird how much more she looked like me than she did her mum. She was a daddy's girl completely.

'Nothing in this world will ever compare to the amount that I love you, Isla.'"

Chapter Sixteen

The fire roared in the Tudor-style living room, though neither Jack nor the cigar-smoking man had put a new log on. The man's whiskey seemed to have the same amount as before, though Jack couldn't determine how that was.

Jack turned and looked behind him. The doorway had disappeared, and instead, Rex was sitting there, surrounded by darkness, in a grand-looking leather armchair, smoking a cigarette, dressed in a black suit. His tie was missing, and the two buttons at the top of his black shirt were undone. A cold beer rested in his left hand.

Jack seriously contemplated whether his drink had been spiked the night before as his confusion derailed the train of all logic. Nothing was making sense to him.

Rex smiled at Jack and drank a few gulps of his beer.

"Rex, my friend, why don't you come and join us?" the man said while pointing to his left. Jack turned. He hadn't noticed that chair before. In fact, he could have sworn it wasn't there.

Rex walked over to the maroon velvet armchair facing the fire, sat, and rested his full pint glass on the table. Jack was confused as to how the pint was so full. It looked as though it had just been poured.

Rex then pulled a cigarette box from his inside pocket and threw it to Jack, who caught it with one hand and then studied the brand logo. He didn't recognise it. *Heavenly.*

Jack opened the box. There was only one cigarette in there and a lighter.

"Don't worry. Have a smoke, close the lid, stick it in your pocket. There'll be another." Rex said with a warm smile on his face. The Man smirked as he sipped on his whiskey. Jack still hadn't drunk any of his.

"Rex, why don't you tell me again what you told me before? I'm sure Jack will want to hear. Just the middle bit, though. Edinburgh can wait for now, and I know you've…

169

somewhere to be." the man suggested calmly with a warm smile before taking a drag of his cigar.

Chapter Seventeen

"That pervert had left me in the middle of a storm, sat on the water without a fucking paddle. Metaphorically speaking, of course. Jesus, Jack… Wanker.

Isla barely said anything on the journey back. Poor girl. Her tears had stopped by the time we'd gotten back to the van. Then, there was a coldness to her. Emotionless. A realisation, I think. A new feeling. Unprecedented. Lonesome and fucking sombre. The shock of it, it would be a lot for anyone to take in, let alone a seven-year-old. It was a different world for her, one she was unprepared for, one I don't think you can prepare for. It all happened so fucking fast; I think she struggled to process it, which is very fucking understandable. Every time I looked over at her as we drove along the country roads away from the woods, I could see that she was frozen in thought, shaken from it. Gazing out the window, not really blinking. Both her mum and her step-mum had been murdered, and then hours later, her dad died in her arms after being shot right in front of her. How would anyone react to that?

Just twenty-four hours before, she was a normal little girl, innocent to the cruelty of the world. She had just experienced and witnessed more heartache and violence than many will ever know in their whole lifetime—all the difference a day makes.

Back at the woods, I called some of my men, men I trusted, to deal with the bodies both at the yard and in the woods. Take them away and make them disappear. They were professionals and had honed an array of skills for dealing with such matters. The same had already been done for the bodies back in Stamford. I told the perverts to get rid of my bike, too. Leave no fucking traces. It will only be a matter of time until the boys in blue start asking perverts questions, and I do not want to be fucking one of them.

'Rex?' said Isla quietly as she looked at the world passing by her window.

'Yes, Little One?' I replied.

'Can we have pancakes?'

'Hmm… That sounds like a good idea. Pancakes it is.'

I thought it would be best to avoid Manchester. I couldn't be fucked for any more drama, not with the little one with me. Fuck knows what horror we could of walked into if Paddy Wang be telling the truth about a war starting out on the streets. Everyone who was anyone around the city knew me—perverts from each corner of the groove. You could hardly miss me. My priority was to keep the little one safe.

I put some petrol in the van at a services, and then drove us to Liverpool. Isla hadn't moved a muscle the whole time.

As we got onto the motorway, I put on the Radio—Smooth Radio—only quietly. I'm not sure if Isla minded; she didn't say anything.

I'd known a lot of perverts to die over the years, but I had just lost a dear friend. The son I never had. It hurt a lot to tell the truth. I chain-smoked the pain away, but I kept it together. I'm not a fucking soft lad.

In Liverpool, we passed a JD. After parking and locking up, I ran in there quick and bought Isla a pair of trainers, some socks and a jumper while she waited in the van. They had just opened up for the day and were over the fucking moon that their first customer had spent nearly two hundred quid on three items.

We drove further into the city centre, parked up, and took a walk to find ourselves a little café. I smoked a couple ciggies on the way. We didn't talk, but Isla stayed close to my side. She knew she was safe with me.

'Pancakes, please. Can I have one with blueberries in and one with chocolate buttons and some maple syrup on the side?' Isla said to the waiter.

'Are ya sure ya don't want da blueberries and buttons mixed together in da same one like?' said the waiter, his scouse accent were strong. Fucking pervert.

Isla turned her head and looked at the waiter. She didn't say anything, but her silent stare said a thousand words. Scared the absolute shit out of the skinny scouse fucker. She wanted what she asked for and nothing else. He understood her look more than I understood that fucking accent of his.

'I'll have a full English and a coffee—black. Get the little one a hot chocolate too—cream, marshmallows and all that.' I said without being asked to ease the tension.

The waiter fucked off, and Isla returned to watching the city come to life out the window. Deliveries were being made. Shop doors were opening. People were walking by with takeaway cups of coffee and dogs on a lead. Shell suit after shell suit. Was like the fucking eighties out there.

'How you feeling, Little One?' I asked her. There was a brief silence while she thought about her answer.

'I don't know… Sad. Too sad to cry, though.'

'My mum and dad died too.' I told her.

'Really? When did you stop feeling sad?'

'We never really get over it. Eventually, It'll get easier. You're allowed to feel sad. It would be weird if you weren't. But know and remember how much the three of them loved you. The best way to honour their love, their lives and their memory is to be the bravest person you can be.'

She was still looking out the window, staring while her mind spiralled and slowly processed everything.

'But… how? How do I make them proud?'

'Well… work hard, then work a little harder, give heart and show a little fire, and stop what's slowing you down. Work hard at school, at everything, everything you put your mind to. It pays to be a winner… And don't worry as well about the people who did this. I'll sort it. They won't be coming back.'

'Are you going to kill them?' Isla asked.

Fuck... What was I supposed to say to that?...

'Most of them are dead already. Your dad and I saw to that. He was a great man, your dad. Do you know his job before you were born? He was in the Parachute Regiment. They're an elite fighting force for the British army. Serious men. The very best. He left the army so that he could be closer to you. Anyway, there's only one more, then they'll all be dead, all the people behind this.'

'I know Daddy's job. He was ferocious.' How the fuck did she know that word?

'Yes. Yes, he was. A fine specimen of a man. A gentleman with honour. Valiant and gallant. A handsome fella, too.' I told her.

'Can I do it?' Isla asked.

'Can you do what? Be a Para?'

'No. Can I get the last one?'

'What do you mean?'

'The last one. Can I shoot them?'

What the fuck? Why would she even think that?

'No. Absolutely not.' I replied. Isla turned her head from looking out the window for the first time. She looked me in the eyes. Her gaze was serious and lacked the path to negotiation.

'Why not?' she asked me.

'Because you're seven.'

'So? I'm nearly eight anyway.' she said confidently.

'So... well, that would be a mental thing to let you do. And no, you're not nearly eight; you've got months until your birthday. No. No, don't you worry yourself about that. You wouldn't be able to cope with the recoil on your little shoulder, let alone fire the shot on target.'

'The position and hold must be firm enough to support the weapon.' Isla said assertively. Why the fuck did she know that?

'What?' I asked.

'The position and hold must be firm enough to support the weapon—the first marksmanship principle. Daddy taught me them. And he taught me to shoot. I can handle the recoil.'

'What? He did what? When?'

'We've always done it. Well, I only got to start firing them when I turned six, but he's always taught me about them. We play with them every week.'

'You've fired a weapon? Your dad taught you to fire a live weapon?'

'Well, not exactly. But he has a toy rifle at home. That's what we use. It fires on a game at the big telly. We practise from different ranges. I can strip an SA80 rifle, too. He taught me. And put it back together. He wouldn't let me play with any live rounds, but I've seen them. They're pretty. I held one once. And I held a Glock 17. I wasn't allowed to tell Mum, though, or Dad said he would get into trouble, and then we wouldn't be able to play with them anymore.'

I were shocked, and that were rare for me. What the fuck, Jack?

'The weapon must point naturally without any undue physical effort.' Isla said confidently. She still refrained from showing any emotion.

'What?' I asked.

'That's the second marksmanship principle.'

'Right...'

'Sight alignment and sight picture must be correct.'

'Any more?' I asked.

'The shot must be released and followed through without any disturbance to the position.'

'Well, I am impressed. Well done, Little One. Bit weird that you know them, but well done.'

That was the first time Isla almost smiled.

'He taught me how to box, too. We would practise Muay Thai. Daddy always let me punch and kick him as hard as I can.'

'I know he did. He told me you were getting good at it. He was a great boxer, your dad. Quick as anything... Did you try and fight the ones who took you last night?'

'No, I was too scared.' Isla said sadly while turning to look out the window again.

'Well, don't you be scared ever again. That would make your daddy proud. Be brave. Always.'

Our breakfast and drinks turned up. Isla must have been starving. She barely stopped to chew. I tucked into my full English. It was good, but I do a better one, and the sausages were a bit shit.

'Rex, who do you have to kill?' Isla asked while halfway through her second pancake, though she hadn't finished her first. I chewed my bit of bacon and swallowed it before having a sip of coffee while I thought over the answer. She'd seen too much and had been through enough to keep these things from her.

'Her name is Alannah. Alannah O'Brien. She's the last one that has the power to hurt us both. Her family runs a gang in Manchester. All of them are dead, apart from her. Once she dies, then all the gang members will either form their own gangs or join others, and their loyalty to the O'Briens will disappear as they won't be getting any money off them. The eldest son of Alannah's, who I shot last night, does have a wife and kids, but I have it under good authority that they're not involved in any way, and they know practically nothing about the family business. Also, the wife is so out of it all the time, off her nut, she doesn't know what day of the week it is.'

'What does out of it mean?'

'She drinks a lot.'

'Mummy drank a lot.'

'Your mum loved you. She was a good woman. She found life hard, but Isla, life is hard. There's no escaping that. But opportunities present themselves. And if you do the easy thing, by being lazy, drinking alcohol all the time, when you're old enough to that is, and sitting round watching pointless tele, then life will become a lot harder. But, if you do the difficult things, like trying at school, getting an education, exercising, reading books and that, boxing and keeping healthy and strong, and putting your time into disciplined tasks, then life will become a little bit easier.

Life is a bit like football. You are your own team. Some days you will lose, and some days you will win. But every day is a new game. It's a new chance to grab life. And as long as you try and win each day, that's all that matters. Some days, you won't win, and that's fine. Failure is important; it teaches us how to improve, how to grow, and how to win the next game. That's what being human is… growth. There are many lessons in losing, and bad days help us appreciate the good. And some days you will win a lot, that's fine too, but don't get too caught up on all that, don't let it get to your head and let it spoil your character, because it will only make you lose the next game.

Your only competition is yourself. Don't worry about what anybody else is doing. Try to be better than the person you were yesterday. Do this each day, and you will go on to achieve monumental success. And don't worry too much about the bad days because they don't last forever. Life isn't linear, and that's fine.

Like a football team, if you are losing a lot, then maybe have a look at the people around you. Get rid of the old players and bring in some new. Surround yourself with winners, people who are better and smarter than you. This way, you will grow. If you surround yourself with losers, then a loser is what you will become.'

Isla looked at me. I could see her little brain ticking away.

'I think I understand.' she said quietly while looking at her pancakes.

'You will do, eventually.'

My phone rang. I got it out my pocket. John was calling.

'Excuse me, Isla, I've got to take this. And I may swear a bit.' I said with a smile.

'Yes, John.' I said after answering the call.

'All sorted?... Good... go on... fucking what?... You fucking what?... Fucking slags... those dirty fucking slags!... Did anyone see anything?... Fuck... fucking hell!... Shithouse... fuck sake... alright, well, just keep to the plan. I'll touch base with ya later on. Watch your back, too; the perverts could be anywhere... alright.'

For fuck sake. Those perverts had only gone and torched my bar. I were fucking fuming. I tried to suppress my anger. I didn't want Isla to see that. But my fucking bar. Gone. Up in smoke. Literally. Fuck sake.

'What's happened?' Isla asked.

'Nothing, Little One. Don't you worry about a thing.'

'Can I do it?' she asked.

'Do what?'

'Shoot her. It would make me feel a lot better. Mummy would be okay with it.'

I thought about it for a moment. I knew I would of wanted to of done the same thing in her position—an eye for an eye. I could see it in her, too. She weren't messing about. She was serious. And, as fucked up as it seemed, it felt almost wrong to take it from her. There's no doubt that the happenings of the previous twenty-four hours would of fucked her up, maybe for life. She were just fucking seven, mate...

My bar, too. Gone. Burned to the ground, John said. Fuck sake. There would be an almighty payout from the insurance company, at least. But that's not the point. All those memories. All those crazy nights and all the bands that had been through that stage. Some of them had gone on to be the real deal. Legends had played there. That was undoubtedly a dark and sad day for the city and the community that we lived among.

All things must pass, though, as George Harrison said. Nothing is truly eternal. Things must come to an end. We had a good run. Twenty-six years, that bar had been bouncing. With that and the money I had made, maybe it was time to retire. I was a very rich man. Maybe it was a sign. I'd gotten that far, and I was still going with all my limbs and a few minor scars. Many were either dead or in prison. Maybe it was meant to be. My time had come to slow down. I'd take the money and disappear. Retirement in… in Cornwall would be nice, I thought. Or Portsmouth or Brighton. Somewhere down south, away from anyone who might know me. Away from all the noise and the chaos of the north.

Also, I was Isla's godfather and the only one still alive. Her life and safety was my responsibility. I could drop her off at Cara's mum's house, but she were fucking mental, and old as fuck. Fuck knows where she lived too.

I took a sip of my coffee and looked at the young girl eating her pancakes.

'Isla, would you like me to drop you off at your nan's house? Do you know where she lives?' I asked her. Isla looked up at me with desperation in her eyes and shook her head.

'No. Please, Rex, No... can I live with you? Please Rex.' begged Isla.

I had promised Jack I would look after her if anything happened to him. I really thought I'd be long gone before him, though.

I thought maybe it would be good for me, would help me settle the fuck down a bit and keep to the retirement idea, keep me on the straight and narrow.

'Okay. Where would you like to live?' I asked her.

'I like the beach.' she replied. The beach?... A lot of chicks at the beach. I didn't mind the sound of that.

'What about Brighton?' I asked.

'Where's Brighton?'

'It's a city down south. Got a big beach, and the weather is almost French.'

'French?... Okay. Can we go on holiday to Paris? Dad and Mindy went there. Mindy said she would take me for my eighth birthday.'

'Okay. We can go to Paris and eat lots of croissants for your birthday. We could go to Disneyland? They have one in Paris.' I took another swig of my coffee.

'No, I don't like Disneyland. I'm not a baby. Rex... can I shoot her?' she asked again. Jesus. Not a baby? I thought about it for a minute.

'I'll tell you what, Little One... You can have one shot. But if you miss, then I'm taking her out.'

'I never miss.' she said seriously without blinking.

'Okay. Then we have a deal. You all finished?'

'Yeah.'

'Okay. Then let's get out of here. We've got to stop off somewhere on the way.'

We left the café and drove back to Manchester, stopping at the supermarket on the way so that I could get a few bits. I had a secret flat on the outskirts of the city that was more of a storage place. No one knew about it, not even John, and I trusted John with my life.

We parked out the back and went inside. We had to get the lift to the fourth floor. I unlocked the front door. I had built a heavy second door two meters behind it. The second door had three padlocks: one at the top, one at the bottom, and one in the middle. After unlocking those, we went in.

The living room was immediately In front of us. It was full of different sorts of gym bags and backpacks that all had different types of weapons and weed in them. A lot of the bags were full of cash, too.

I had two other places like that. One was a flat in Leeds, and one was a house in a village called Essendine, not far from Stamford. Jack also used the one in Essendine. That one had a lot of cash in it and a few guns but no weed or pills. Jack avoided that part of the business.

The dust made Isla sneeze.

'Make yourself comfy for a minute. Careful what you touch. And Isla... please keep away from the window.' I told her, even though there was literally no furniture to sit on.

I went into the bathroom with the carrier bag I got from the supermarket. Out of the bag, I pulled out some shaving gel, a razor, and a pair of scissors. I ran the hot tap and wiped the mirror above the bathroom basin clean before picking up the scissors, and then I started trimming away at my moustache. Once the hair was short enough, I stuck the shaving foam all over the bottom of my face, neck, and the top of my head and shaved the whole lot off.

I hadn't seen myself without a moustache since I was fifteen. Good looking bastard, I thought to myself as I stared back at my shaven reflection. No one would of recognised me. Not even my mother. God rest her soul.

Then, I pulled out a baseball cap and a long-sleeve black T-shirt from the carrier bag and put both on before walking out to the living room.

Isla was shocked, and her reaction wasn't as kind as my own. But at least she was laughing again.

Isla waited in the flat while I made a couple trips back and forth to the van outside to load it up with a few bags of cash. Then, back in the flat, I pulled out a couple of rifles, SA80s, and got Isla to show me what she knew.

She hadn't been lying. She stripped and cleaned the weapons confidently and performed a function test with them both. Then, she got into the prone position and went through the nine-point checklist for firing from the prone.

She relaxed both her legs, then positioned the butt of the rifle firmly and comfortably into her right shoulder, then she secured her left-hand grip and her left elbow position, then her right-hand grip and her right elbow position. Then she moved her head and relaxed it before a noticeable change occurred in her breathing. She stayed like that for a moment, silent and confident.

'Okay, Isla. But you still only get one shot.' I told her. She turned around to me with a massive look of excitement and gratitude on her face.

'I can shoot Alannah?' she asked.

'Yes.'

'Thank you, Rex!'

We got back into the van and drove to the opposite side of the city and then to the outskirts, where the O'Brien's farm was. We parked half a mile away from the farm and walked the rest on foot through the fields.

It was a beautiful day. The sun was shining, and the weather was warm. Birds flew above us in a sky with barely any clouds. A gentle breeze blew as we treaded through the grass. Both of us got a little sweat on. I was smoking a ciggie and had a gym bag on my back. Inside it was two rifles and nine magazines, all fully loaded with ammunition.

Near the farm's perimeter, we ducked down behind a tree. I pulled out both weapons, and we each made a rifle loaded and ready. I stuck a magazine in each of my back pockets and hid the gym bag in the bush.

'Okay, so you know the plan?' I whispered to her.

'Yep.' she said with a little laugh.

'What's funny?'

'Your top lip. You look funny without your moustache.'

'Ha, Ha… Come on, Little One, let's go.'

We continued to the farmhouse's garden. Alannah was there. I could see her. She had her back to us, in the garden, on her own, drinking tea and reading the newspaper at a table in the sun. A lit ciggie was resting in her right hand, that she was slowly smoking, pretending to read the paper while mourning the death of her sons. She can't of known for certain all the details of what happened, but she would of known enough. The rest she could work out. She'd lived in the gangster's world long enough; she knew how things went.

Isla and I crouched silently into the prone. We were about a hundred meters away, maybe less.

'Okay, Isla. You've got one shot. If you don't take her out, then I will, and then we'll get the hell out of here.' I whispered.

'Okay, Slim.' she whispered back.

'What? Who?'

'Slim Shady… One shot.'

'How the hell do you know who that is?' I said. She giggled quietly.

We both aimed at her head with our rifles. We were going for the kill shot. I watched Alannah through my scope as she sat smoking in the sun. The cross of my scope fixed on her long hair. No one else was around, not for miles, I was certain.

'Whenever you're ready.' I whispered to Isla.

'Got it.' she whispered back.

Isla was on my left side. I opened my left eye and could see her out the corner of my view. Her breathing began to slow. She took a big deep breath in and then exhaled, then another deep breath, and then exhaled again, deflating her lungs completely. I closed my left eye and got ready to shoot.

There was no need to be nervous; I never was, ever. If Isla missed, I wouldn't of had long until Alannah had moved to the safety of some sort of cover after hearing the missed shot, and I was confident that was how it was gonna play out. I wouldn't miss though.

I teased my finger over the trigger. My safety was off, and my scope was fixed onto Alannah's head. Those fucking O'Brien's. My fucking bar, mate.

Gunfire blasted through my left ear, and the birds fled the area in distress. For a split second, I couldn't see if Isla had missed or not. I got ready to pull the trigger. My finger was just about to squeeze, and then I saw it. I saw Alannah fall to her side through my scope. Her head fell and hung to her left over the side of the chair, and blood started to drip from her skull onto the patio. She'd done it.

'Got her!' Isla whispered excitedly.

'Good drills, Little One. How's your shoulder?'

'It's fine.' Isla said happily.

'Good drills. Proper. Right, let's get out of here.'

We doubled back towards the gym bag that I had left behind the bush and put the weapons in before continuing to run back to the van. I started the ignition, and we drove away at speed.

We used the country roads for a while until we got far enough away from the city to feel safe from any police presence. Then we headed south. Brighton was our destination.

'How do you feel?' I asked Isla after driving for nearly an hour. She had been sat quietly, looking out the passenger window as we drove down the motorway. Smooth Radio was on again, of fucking course.

'I'm not sure. Still really sad. But I'm happy that you let me take the shot. Thank you, Rex.'

'You're welcome, Little One. Your dad would be very proud of you, very proud. All of them would be…

Once we get to Brighton, I'll have to use my legal name, Ronnie. I haven't been called that since I were eleven. Even my old dear used to call me Rex. Too many people know

me, though, and Rex isn't exactly a very common name…
You can have a new name, too, if you like. What would
you like to be called?'

The young girl paused before answering. I could sense
the clogs turning in her brain as she watched the cars we
passed through the window. Then she replied with a degree
of certainty.

'Isla Jack.'"

Chapter Eighteen

"2022.

Brighton was alright. Isla settled in nicely to her new school. She'd been there for over a year. She hadn't made many friends, but she was doing well, working hard. All her teachers thought she were the fucking bollocks. Thrilled they were whenever I saw them, telling me how clever she was, or how good a reader she were, or what a joy she was to teach. They were a little concerned that she sat on her own at lunch, but Isla said it didn't bother her.

'I like just sitting and reading at lunch. The other kids just talk about dumb stuff. They run around like crazy people, shouting and screaming. It's a bit odd.' Isla told me. It were mad to think she were only nine years old a few weeks back.

I was enjoying retirement, rather a fucking lot too. I'd wake up, sort Isla with breakfast and drive her to school. Then while she were there I'd hit the gym. Smash it. I'd kick the shit out of a bag a few times a week, too, keep my fighting tricks in good nick and let off a little steam. Then I'd have a spot of lunch down the pub—a couple pints of Guinness. I'd take the dog with me. We got a white Labrador. A beautiful little boy. Just a pup. Isla named him Duke. She thought it were funny; said Mindy would tell her how she thought her dad had a dog's name. I'd take Duke for a walk down the seafront; then we'd go pick the little one up from school. Isla cracked on with her schoolwork. I cooked dinner. Fucking sorted, mate. Then, in the evening, I'd take Duke for another little walk.

Every day I'd have a little sit down at the table with Isla for about an hour. Maybe during dinner, sometimes after. It was a space to let her unwind and to try and teach her a couple of things, things I'd picked up along the way. Ideologies, history, finance, life expectations, the power of positive thinking. Most of all, I'd try and inspire her to grow and encourage her to do well. I'd let her unload on me, too, on how she were feeling. She was weirdly coping with all the shit that happened the year before pretty well. I could see it was still hurting her, though. Often, she did get a little upset, had a little cry. That was understandable. But the past couple months, she'd been golden.

I'd get a full rundown on how her day went at school— all her classes and what she'd learned. It was good to see her smile, but she didn't do it very often. Most of the time, she'd be pretty serious. I managed to make her laugh a few times, but it were often by accident, and usually if I'd fucked something up. She were always correcting me, telling me to say 'have' instead of 'of', and 'are' instead of 'is' if it's plural.

She had a few photos with her mum, dad, and Mindy. They were precious to her. I don't know what she did with them; I think they were in her room somewhere. But I know she thought about the three of them a lot.

Isla read everything, just like Mindy. It was a good way for her to escape, I think. I was having to buy her a new book nearly every fucking week. I didn't mind, though.

We didn't have a tele, but I got us both posh new iPads. I'd read that I should have probably been managing her screen time, but I didn't need to. She was more interested in books and learning to fight than she was anything else. Obsessed. And she seemed to be obsessed with getting enough sleep, too. She were always telling me I needed to get more sleep. Fuck knows what time she went to bed, but she was always up and full of energy the next day. More than I were, anyway.

For an hour, three times a week, I'd give her one-on-one boxing lessons in the second bedroom upstairs. That was the only time I went up there really. She were fucking good. Quick hands. A mega punch and kick on her. I'd put the pads on and let her go at me. I think it helped her.

Helped her to release a lot of the anger she felt about the way they all died. Helped her to feel safer. She needed not worry, though. I wasn't going to let fuck all happen to her.

Our house was pretty fucking mega. A cosy little thing. She had the upstairs all to herself, and I had the down. I liked my little set-up. I'd got my own toilet and bathroom downstairs, as she did too upstairs with the ensuite. The living room was actually my bedroom. Me and Duke guarded the gaff at night.

I told her she had to keep it tidy up there, and if not, then, well, she'd have to live in a shit tip. The girl seemed to be pretty good with all that. Kept asking me for a new can of fucking polish every month. Fucking polish? I didn't fuck about with shit like that downstairs. What do you think I am, some sort of fucking polish pervert? I did hoover though, fucking mad for it with the hoover. See a crumb, fucking right on it.

On Saturdays, we'd do something—go to a museum, go shopping, or something similar—often in a different city. We'd take Duke if we could. Isla loved Duke; he was her best friend. Then, if we were back in time, we'd go out for a meal at night.

Sundays, we went the same place every week for a roast. Duke was, of course, always definitely there for that. Isla hated leaving him on his own. Then, Sunday afternoons, Isla sorted out what she needed for the week ahead. Did her washing and Ironing and that. I had to get a YouTube tutorial video up to teach us both how to iron. I never really fucked about with shit like that before—had been years. I paid someone to do all that for me. Those days, however, were long gone. Was trying to keep a low profile. Didn't want perverts coming in and out the gaff.

There were still fucking plants everywhere. Aloes and money plants, peace lilies and a cactus, too. Isla got on board. She started planting shit in the back garden. Fuck knows what. I didn't fuck about with flowers. I took her to a garden centre, and she picked what seeds she wanted—seemed to make her happy. She was in her element, watering and feeding them every day.

We were safe. Everything was fine… And then we weren't…

It happened one night in the week, around one in the morning. I was up, re-reading Sun Tzu's 'The Art of War'. Duke became restless. He was up and poking his nose about by the window. At first, I thought it were nothing. But then I heard something. I checked the CCTV on the iPad. I had a camera out the front and round the back. There were three geezers hanging about by the front door, tryna get in.

I got up out my chair and, walked over, and gave Duke a rub on the head. Then I left my room and closed the door behind me. I still had my boots on—old habit. I quietly walked through the house. All the lights were off apart from a reading lamp in my bedroom. I grabbed a baseball bat that was next to the front door and stood ready.

The three men were trying their best to be quiet, but they were making a lot of noise fucking about trying to get the door open. The men obviously weren't professionals. I thought about getting my rifle, but I didn't yet know who the perverts were. Maybe it wasn't personal. Maybe they were just local thieves. I didn't like the thought of killing them over something so trivial as just breaking an entry. No. I would kick the absolute shit out of them instead.

Also, they could have been police. I didn't need them lot knowing I'd got live firearms in the gaff.

The lock to the front door clicked. They'd picked it. Fuck, I knew I should have put an extra bolt on that door. Still, I needed to know who the perverts were.

The front door slowly opened. The first man quietly took a step in. I flicked the kitchen light on, the room the front door opened onto. The geezer shat himself, mate. Should have seen the size of him compared to me. Tiny little fucker. A middle-aged white geezer in a tracksuit.

'Coulda just knocked, mate.' I told him. Then I swung the bat round his face. Knocked him clean out. Might have hit him a little too hard to be honest. I didn't have time to bother myself with that; the other two were already in and kicking off.

We began to fight. Two on one. These pair were younger than the first. A couple white lads, again in tracksuits. One of them were like a fucking ninja, had a few tattoos on his neck. He hit me twice round the face at lightning speed and then kicked me round the side of the head. How the fuck did he get his leg up there? I took it like a champ and hit him in the face with a left jab, which knocked him back a few steps. Then I swung the bat to hit him round the head just as the other standing geezer swung his fist for my face. The ninja pervert blocked the bat with his forearm and moaned in pain as he caught it.

Then, the other geezer pulled out a knife. I quickly stomped down on the knife fella's knee with the bottom of my boot while the ninja matey right hooked me round the face again. I released my right-hand grip on the bat, keeping it in my left, and punched the ninja in the face before grabbing the bat again with both hands and swinging it at the knife-holding hand of the other man. The knife fell to the ground, and then I side-kicked him in the stomach. He went flying.

The ninja jumped on my back, like a piggyback pervert, tryna fucking strangle me from behind. I smashed myself backwards a few steps and hit the wall behind me so the ninja would take the full brunt of it. It didn't work; he was still hanging on and trying to choke me out.

The knife fella was up and punched me in the face twice. I could feel blood from my nose starting to pour down my face. I kicked out and caught the knife pervert in the chest.

He flew backwards, lost his balance and hit the ground hard.

Then I smashed backwards into the wall behind me again and twatted the back of my head into the ninja's face at the same time. Still, he was holding on.

I decided to put all my effort into doing a front somersault. I threw the bat to the side, squatted slightly and grabbed onto his hands at the front of my neck to keep them there. Then I pushed off hard and landed the somersault on my back with the ninja beneath me. It hurt, but I knew it hurt him a hell of a lot more than it did me. One hundred- and fifteen kilograms landing on top of you doesn't tickle, mate.

The man who had the knife had picked up the baseball bat and started hitting me in the stomach with it while I were lying on top of the ninja geezer. He kept swinging, hitting me and hitting me, so I flung my legs round and kicked his feet from beneath him. He hit the floor and smacked his head on the ground as he landed. I rolled over and hammer-punched him in the face. Knocked him out cold. Two of them were out of it.

The ninja was groaning on the floor. I think I'd broken one of his ribs. Credit to him, he were still awake, not like the other two.

I got up, grabbed him by his collar and pulled him to his feet. Then I wrapped my hands around his neck and shoved him up against the wall.

'Who sent you!? Who the fuck are ya!?' I shouted at the man. He didn't reply; he just squirmed. Still holding his neck, I lifted him from the ground.

'You've got five seconds to tell mc. Who sent you here?'

He continued to squirm as his trainers dangled; they weren't touching the ground.

Then there was gunfire.

I turned around while still holding the ninja by the neck. The first man that I knocked out with the bat was standing there with a knife in his hand. He dropped the knife and fell to the floor while holding his chest. Blood started pouring out of his wound, and he began to choke.

Isla appeared with a loaded Glock 17 in her hand.

'Where'd you get that from?' I asked her. I were shocked, mate, truly.

'One of your bags. I've had it for a while. I'm sorry. I wanted it to feel safe. You're not mad, are you?' she replied in a high-pitched voice, scared that she had let me down. It was hard to be mad at her. I still had my hands wrapped around the ninja's neck.

'No, Little One, I'm not mad. But next time, ask first, okay? Jesus. Nice shot anyway.' I replied. She smiled.

I turned my attention to the ninja who I had up against the wall.

'A little girl just shot your mate. You best tell me what I wanna know 'cause we ain't fucking about.'

I looked deep into the ninja's eyes. He looked scared. I loosened my grip slightly to let him talk.

'Cut off one head, and two will grow back. The O'Brien's are a big family. They are coming for you, for you both.' the ninja said through struggled breath.

'How did you find us?'

'It wasn't all that hard. Everyone has a price. Be careful with your trust.' he said while smirking. That pissed me off, so I headbutted him in the face and broke his fucking nose. Blood and tears poured down onto his chin while he groaned. Some of his blood fell onto my hands. I didn't like that. Fucking irritated the fuck out of me, if I'm honest. I were meant to be retired.

'Who gave us up?' I demanded.

Then I heard the original knife man, who I had knocked out with the hammer punch, start to come around. He was slowly waking up. I turned to look at him, still holding the ninja's neck up against the wall.

A second shot was fired.

'Jesus, Isla, can you stop shooting people, please?'

She had shot the pervert on the ground at near enough point-blank range in the head.

'I'm sorry. I didn't like the look of him. He scared me.' she said nervously.

'How did he scare you?'

'He moved his head.'

'Fucking hell.' I turned my attention back to the ninja.

'She's shot both your mates. Before that, I took on the three of ya. There's only you left. It's not looking very good. Now, do you want to fucking die, mate?'

'Fuck you, Rex.' the ninja said. I head-butted him in the face again. The ninja cried out in pain.

'Fuck! That one hurt. Ah shit! Ahhh!' he moaned.

'Do you want a third?'

'No, No, No, you're alright. Look, I don't know anything. We were just sent here to do you in. I don't know who it was that gave you up, I just know someone did, alright. That's all I know. Just let me go, and I'll fuck off. I won't say a word.' the ninja insisted.

'I think you're fucking lying, mate. What say you, Isla? Reckon he's lying?'

'He's lying.' she replied confidently.

'I'm not; I'm not. I swear. Honest.'

I punched him in the gut hard and took a step back.

'I'll tell you what I'm gonna do. I'm gonna count to five, and if you haven't told me what I wanna know by five, then this little girl is gonna shoot you in the fucking face, mate. Alright? Alright. One… Two… Three…'

Then there was the sound of gunfire again.

'Isla for fuck sake… I said five! Jesus. I was gonna grab him again at four and try and get some more out of him… Christ alive.'

'I'm sorry. I got a bit excited.'

'Fucking hell… It's fine. It's fine. Ahh, bloody hell… Christ alive… I liked this place as well… Right, Isla, pack your things, all the things you want to take with you. We've gotta get going.'

'Where are we going?'

'I don't know yet. We'll talk about it in the car.'

'Are we taking Duke?'

'Yes, we're taking Duke. Now go on, get your things together. And make that gun safe too; there'll be no more shooting tonight, okay?'

Isla smiled and unloaded her Glock while running upstairs and packing her things together. I stood back and looked at the three dead men on the ground. Fucking hell. Someone's bound to have heard that—stupid perverts.

Back in my room, Duke was hiding, scared, under the bed.

'Well, at least you being a bit of a wimp balances things out between the three of us.' I said to him while stroking him under the chin.

Once my bags were packed, I loaded both mine and Isla's stuff into the back of the car. I'd only got the car a few months back. It was a red Toyota Hilux. I loved it.

The three of us got in. Duke was on Isla's lap. Then we drove off away from the house and away from the city.

If it be true what that ninja pervert at the house was talking about before Isla shot him, then we needed to be double careful not to be found again. The O'Brien's were still onto us, and they were not gonna stop. I thought Edinburgh might have been a good place to drive to next.

At least we were safe for the time being. We would keep each other safe, the three of us—watch each other's backs. I was obligated to find a way for Isla to live a decent life that directed her and prepared her for success. It was my duty. It might not have been a normal one, but an extraordinary life is never something to fear. And even if it was, we would have felt the fear and done it anyway."

Chapter Nineteen

The rain continued to pelt down on the window. Both Rex and the armchair he was sitting in had disappeared in the blink of an eye, though his cold pint of lager remained on the table. For the first time, the fire looked to be burning out, diminishing the light around the room.

The cigar-smoking man smiled knowingly and spoke.

"Jack, don't worry about him. It was just a... flying visit.

I enjoyed our little chat, though I'm afraid I must go now, too. You can use the door behind me to leave, when you're ready that is. No rush. Take all the time you need, but you'll find that time does turn a little... differently around here...

Unless I'm mistaken, someone is waiting for you on the other side of the door with a couple of cocktails. Porn star martinis, I believe."

Author email: AuthorNathanWilson@outlook.com

Printed in Great Britain
by Amazon

47657734R10111